AVALA

SPIRITS OF THE
MINDSCAPES

BOOK 1: HOPE

[signature]

Caleb Teal

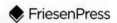 FriesenPress

Suite 300 - 990 Fort St
Victoria, BC, V8V 3K2
Canada

www.friesenpress.com

Copyright © 2019 by Evelon II Studios
First Edition — 2019

www.authorcalebteal.com
www.eveloniistudios.com

Edited by Cindy Girard

ISBN
978-1-5255-5481-0 (Hardcover)
978-1-5255-5482-7 (Paperback)
978-1-5255-5483-4 (eBook)

1. FICTION, SCIENCE FICTION, ADVENTURE

Distributed to the trade by The Ingram Book Company

This book is dedicated to:
My young cat, Tracer Racer,
who I love very much
and who loves me back
more than anyone.

Also dedicated to:
My best friend, Stephanie
My younger brother, Christopher
My mother, Cindy
My father, Wayne
And my two elder cats, Niffy and Midou,
who have all been very supportive of me over the years

PART 1

-BEGINNING-

1

ATHAKARIN

Avala hated what she saw. It sickened her to the core. What they were doing was wrong. However, it was the only way to appease the spirits, or so the priests would have everyone believe.

Avala watched in horror as the man on the altar was burned alive. Her round amber eyes took in the gruesome spectacle as tears trickled down her pale cheeks. A lock of her golden hair fell in front of her face, blocking her vision for a moment before she swept it aside. She had to see this. If she did not, it could anger the spirits, and that would negate the sacrifice.

She watched in somber anger until all that was left was a charred husk. Finally, the elder priest raised the symbol of Yasal and recited the words of old. "May the spirits forgive our trespasses. May Yvan and Ijar turn away from our transgressions. May the death of this soul not be in vain. May we have peace from the wrath of punishment. May Yasal grant us mercy. May our sacrifice be accepted." With that, the ceremony came to a close. Avala left the temple as quickly as possible, wanting to forget the horrors that she witnessed there.

Outside the sky was dark, as always, the stars twinkling in the void. The eternal fires to the west illuminated the horizon. She hurried through the cold to her home on the east edge of town, hugging her cloak close to her body. When she arrived at her hut, she kicked open the door, shattering the ice that had formed on it, and stormed inside.

She lit the hearth and then lay down on the pillows next to it. Only then did she finally release the wellspring of tears hidden within her. Her brother was the man who had been burned in the temple, burned to appease the wrath of imaginary spirits, because the people of her village were too enslaved to tradition to realize the spirits did not exist.

The door, which was still open, slammed shut. She didn't even bother to see why, for she knew who had closed it: her husband, who she had been forced to marry when she was eight. She hated him, just like she hated the priests, but she was too afraid to lash out. She knew there was nowhere to flee if she did. To the east was frozen wastelands and to the west eternal fire. To the north and south were more villages, all following the same laws and worshipping the same made-up spirits. She was trapped in a hell worse than anything the priests could dream up.

"I was worried about you, Avala," her husband said softly.

"As if you actually care what happens to me!" she replied through her sobs.

"Of course I do. You know as well as I do that these sacrifices are wrong!"

"No you don't! If you did you wouldn't have taken me from my parents!" This was the first time she had ever shown any sign of disliking of her forced marriage. It was a punishable offense for a woman to refuse the man she was given to, but she didn't care anymore.

"When your parents deemed you were ready for a husband, I ensured that you came to me to protect you from what some of the other men might do to you. You know I have never laid a hand on you against your will. I have tried to treat you with kindness, which most women are not afforded."

"You're not going to beat me, like what father did to mother?" she asked, utterly confused.

He looked at her incredulously. "I would never treat a woman that way." He shook his head and sighed. "Why have I been forced to live on this barbaric world for so long?"

Avala tilted her head in confusion, "What was that?"

"Avala, I . . . I come from another world. I am not Athakarin like you. I was sent here to watch and observe."

"Then what are you?" she asked, the tears receding from her eyes. She had always wondered why Alvaj had never treated her like her father treated her mother. She assumed it was just some sort of torture he was putting her through, to see how long until she broke. That's how men treated women. It was the way things were.

"We call ourselves human. We're here to end the cruel reign of another off-worlder who calls herself Yasal. Her kind is the bitter enemy of my people," he said, his hands behind his back.

She leaped to her feet. "All these years, and you never told me? You could have saved Vran! Couldn't you? And . . . and Yasal isn't real! The spirits aren't real!" She didn't know what was worse, the fact that she wanted to believe him or the possibility that he was just trying to torment her.

"Avala, I tried to save your brother, but the priests got to him first. I am forbidden from attacking the natives unless ordered. To do so would reveal ourselves to Yasal."

She stared at him. He couldn't be from another world. He looked so much like any other man, except . . . she had never seen anyone with blue eyes before. She studied his eyes. The more she looked at them, the more she realized they did not seem Athakarin. The pupils were the wrong shape; instead of slits, they were circles. Why didn't she notice this before? She could have sworn they weren't like this in the past.

She gasped. The Devalra were said to have round pupils, at least when they took the form of mortals. The priests claimed they were evil spirits who delighted in destroying those loyal to Yasal. The Athakarin were said to be the offspring of the good spirits, the Yaji, and the evil spirits, the Devalra. It was because of this mixed heritage that mortals existed. Due to that evil side of their heritage, Yasal required constant sacrifices to appease her. Could it be that her people were actually the descendants of two different beings from other worlds, beings who were stuck in a war?

"Are you a Devalra?" she asked shyly.

"That is what the Yajirans call us," he replied, "but I assure you that we do not seek to enslave your people, like they do. We seek freedom and equality for all."

Avala eyed him suspiciously. "I should tell the priests."

"The priests are just going to demand you give yourself as a sacrifice once I escape. You are better off coming with me."

"Coming with you where?" she asked with sudden excitement. Was he offering her a chance to leave this hell behind? Perhaps she had misjudged him. When she looked at him, all she used to see was a man who was just as cruel and unforgiving to women as any other on her world. Now she didn't know what she saw, but he was suddenly fascinating, a mystery to be solved.

"I'm leaving my post on this world and going back to headquarters," he said. "I've been given permission to take you with me—for your protection."

She knew what he meant. If a man left a woman, it was essentially a death sentence. Without the ability to get a job, she would starve within a month. She would also be up for grabs by any other man in town, and she hated the way most of them looked at her. This was her chance to leave it all behind—if he was telling the truth. However much she wanted to believe him, it seemed too unlikely.

What do I have to lose by trusting him? If he's just trying to break me more, there's nothing I can do. But if he's telling the truth . . ..

"I would like to go with you," she said finally.

"Good. We leave at the ninth bell. Make certain you have everything you want to bring with you. We won't be able to come back for anything."

She retrieved the few belongings that mattered to her and placed them in a pack. They included her Mohavji necklace, which she received from her mother right before her death. She also packed her red Knakta crystal, which she found when she was a child, and her seven birth rings, each of which each signified something about her birth. Alvaj said they would not need food for the trip, but she packed some anyway: two loaves of Milic bread, baked the previous cycle.

When the town bells tolled nine times, she was ready to go. Alvaj grabbed her hand unexpectedly. She tried to pull it away, but before she could, the world around her melted away. She was suddenly in a brightly lit room with metal walls and floors. Alvaj released her hand as she looked around at the alien room.

She checked below her and saw that she was standing on a large disk stuck to the floor. It was big enough to fit at least eight people standing close together. The walls of the round room were adorned with big rectangular panels made of the same glowing material as the plate. On one side of the room was a door, which slid open to both sides as Alvaj approached.

Avala followed Alvaj into a large chamber filled with strange furniture and people. As she entered, they all stared at her. A woman stepped forward. She looked like one of Avala's people except for her eyes and her strange outfit. Instead of a robes, tunic, or cloak, she wore a white form-fitting outfit with a gold stripe down the right side.

"Greetings, Agent Allan. I see she took you up on your offer," the woman said to Alvaj before turning to Avala. "You must be Avala. I am Commander Sylvia of the Earth Intelligence Service. Let me be the first to welcome you to the planet of Hydra Three."

"Is . . . this . . . real?" Avala asked softly. Everything around her was white. The other people wore the same white form-fitting outfits as Sylvia, although the stripes came in a variety of colors. Some were blue, some red, and others green or gold. Flashing lights of many different colors blinked around the room. It was like she was in a palace for spirits.

"Amazing, isn't it?" Sylvia said as she watched Avala take it in. "We call this the command center."

Suddenly, it occurred to Avala that Sylvia had claimed she was a commander, a position of authority. *That couldn't be what she meant, could it?* "Are you . . . in charge?" she asked shyly.

"Of everything that happens here, yes. There are others who I have to answer to, but . . .." She paused, as if shocked at a sudden revelation. "Given your people's poor treatment of women, you must be surprised to see a woman in charge. Is that it?"

Avala nodded.

"No need to worry. Among our people, men and women are treated as equals. The only thing that puts me in charge of others is my rank, which I had to earn. I'm certain you'll like that about us." She paused to address Alvaj. "Agent Allan, you are dismissed. Make yourself presentable, and then report for debriefing." Sylvia turned back to Avala. "As for you, let me take you to your new home. Please, follow me."

Avala followed her through a doorway and along twisting white hallways until she stopped at a door. She touched the side of the door, and it opened. Sylvia motioned for Avala to step inside. As soon as she did, she noticed the interior looked similar to the home that she had just left behind. However, a strange device was set into the far wall. And though the windows looked real, when she tried to put her hand through one, she hit an invisible wall.

"It's an illusion, dear," Sylvia said. "We call them holograms." She pointed to the device in the wall. "If you need anything, such as food or heat, just talk to the Adjutant. That's what we call the device on the wall. Also, don't try lighting the fire the normal way. Just ask the Adjutant." She smiled. "I'll be back in the command center. Feel free to look around the complex. If you get lost, just ask any of the adjutants you see for help."

As Sylvia turned to leave, Avala grabbed her arm and put her forehead to Sylvia's wrist in a sign of gratitude. Tears streamed down her face. "Thank you for this great gift of freedom."

Sylvia put her hand on Avala's head. "You're welcome, child." Then she left, the door sliding closed behind her.

2

A NEW LIFE

Avala opened her pack, which had been on her back the entire time. She took out her belongings and placed them beside the hearth pillows. Then she placed the bread in the pantry. Now she understood why they did not need food for the journey. She went over to the hearth and picked up the flint lighter. Before she could use it, a voice spoke from the wall.

"Please, do not use fire starters in the complex. Doing so is prohibited by regulation 2599.3."

Avala jumped and spun around to face the strange device. A picture of a woman's face was on the previously blank panel. She stared at it, partly in fear and partly in awe.

"If you desire the hearth lit, please let me know. Since it is only a third-level hologram, it will act like fire in every way other than burning the structure or people. The same cannot be said of real fire."

Avala nodded, hoping that was enough. Suddenly, the hearth lit up in flames, warmth radiating from it. She barely noticed; all she could do was stare at that face on the device. She had never seen anything like it.

"Please, do not be afraid of me. I am the Adjutant designated: EIS. I am a fully self-aware artificial intelligence, hired to act as an aid to all personnel in the complex. If you require anything, just ask. If you require privacy, press the blue button at the bottom of the panel. Press it again when you need me."

Avala shook her head as if to clear away the insanity of all that was happening. "Where's Alvaj?" she asked.

"Agent Allan, code-named Alvaj, is in debriefing. He has left a message for you. Do you wish to hear it?"

She nodded. Suddenly, a transparent version of Alvaj materialized in front of the device. "Avala, this is a recorded message that is unable to respond to your voice, so please, don't try. I wanted to inform you that due to laws prohibiting forced marriages within the Republic of Earth, you and I are no longer married. You are a free woman—free to do what you want. Laws in the Republic allow you to do things you wouldn't have been able to before because of your gender. You can get a job, and you can say no to men, among other things.

"However there are some things you must know. If someone tries to hurt you or threaten you, they are breaking the law. You not only have the right but also the responsibility to report them—even if the person is a man. Also, because of your race, Commander Sylvia has an interest in using you in the war against the Yajirans. I wanted to make certain you know that if she asks for your assistance, you have the right to refuse. She cannot force you, since you are not part of the military or the intelligence agency. However, if you do aid her, you might be able to help more of your people. I'm glad you chose to come with me. I wish you well. Alvaj out." With that the hologram faded.

Avala had tears in her eyes. She was truly free, free of a lifetime of fear and sadness. Up until six years earlier, she had thought she could handle it. That was when her parents gave her to Alvaj. She had hated him because of that, because he had taken her from her family. From her mother, who died shortly afterward. From her older brother, the only man she knew who did not see her as a plaything.

From her father. Even though she hated him more than anyone, he never actually hurt her like he did other women.

Now the only one left was her father, and she was glad she never had to see him again. She was glad that that village was behind her now; however, the horrors of her youth would haunt her forever. If she had a chance to make things right, to save her people, would she take it? Maybe for the other women. But the men? Did they deserve saving? No, and yet her brother had treated women fairly. Maybe there were more men like him.

She shook her head, trying to clear away the thoughts of the past. She was a free person now. Dwelling on the past would not help. But she couldn't let go, not yet. She needed to understand why her people were the way they were. Was she truly descended from these humans and Yajirans? If so, why were her people so obviously primitive? These humans possessed magic far beyond what the mages of the Northlands could wield.

"Where did my people come from?" she asked the seemingly dormant device.

The face of the Adjutant reappeared. "The Athakarin are the descendants of the human inhabitants of Evelon II and rebel Yajirans who took refuge there. The Yajiran rebels called themselves Athakri. While the first children of the humans and Athakri were still infants, the Yajiran high council discovered their location and sent five of their Yajixa to eliminate them. The—"

"What are the Yajixa?" Avala asked.

"The Yajixa are the special agents of the Yajirans. They have learned how to transfer their consciousness to new bodies, which allows them to prolong their life almost indefinitely. It also makes them nearly impossible to kill. The Republic of Earth has yet to discover their secret, since all Yajixa are fiercely loyal and extremely secretive." The Adjutant paused. "May I continue with your first information request, or shall I treat the query as answered?"

Avala nodded, then realized that did not answer the question. "Please continue."

"Very well. After the Yajixa arrived on the planet, they eliminated the humans and the Yajiran rebels. However, the Yajixa have laws preventing them from slaying children, so all children on the planet, including the half-human/half-Yajiran children, were raised by the Yajixa known as Yagra."

Avala gasped. Yagra was the Mother Spirit, the one who was said to watch over infants and pregnant mothers.

"When the pure Yajiran among the children came of age," the Adjutant continued, "they were taken by Yasal, the leader of the Yajixa Generals of Evelon II. She trained them in the ways of the Yajixa. However, when the pure humans came of age, they were executed immediately. Although the half-Yajirans were also half-human, the Yajixa decided not to execute them and instead rule over them like gods, as they have done with countless other primitive species. They intend to raise them up against the humans and their allies, when they became advanced enough. All this happened two thousand years ago."

Avala was shocked. Athakarins only lived around ninety years. For Yasal and the others to still be around, they would have transferred their consciousness over a dozen times. That is, assuming the Yajirans lived as long as Athakarins did, which, now that she thought of it, was not the best assumption to make.

"What happened to the five Yajixa?"

"Current intelligence suggests Yasal is inhabiting the body of Mage Queen Yamlai of the Northlands. Ijar is possessing Fire King Vluad of Avraintix. Yagra has recently taken over Amalix, the wife of the Fire King in the city of Avraintix. Zayil's current identity is unknown. However, it is assumed he has taken the form of a lowly beggar in the City of Ruins, as he often does. And Yvan has taken over the body of Priest Daigix of Childya Village."

"Daigix!" Avala let out a scream of panic. Her village was the village of Childya, and Daigix was the one who had sacrificed her brother. She was angry now. Daigix was one of the spirits in disguise, and it was because of him that her brother was dead. He had sacrificed Vran to himself and his people.

"Indeed. You came from Childya, did you not?" the Adjutant replied.

"He killed my brother! He killed Vran!" she shouted, her anger turning to sobs.

A while later, a strange beeping sound came from a panel next to the door, momentarily distracting her from her emotions. "Avala, it's me, Sylvia. May I come in?"

"I guess so," Avala replied, uncertain if she could be heard. However, a moment later, the door slid open, and Sylvia stepped inside, the door sliding shut behind her.

"I hope you're settled in," Sylvia said softly. "I have a proposition for you, if you'd like to hear it."

Avala nodded for her to continue.

"The Adjutant informed me that you know enough of the current situation on your world. I would like to offer you an invitation to join the fight against the Yajirans."

"I don't know how I could help you. I don't know how to fight." Avala lowered her head shyly.

"We have ways around that. The Yajirans may have figured out ways to transfer consciousness, but we have figured out how to grant knowledge and experience to those who don't have it almost instantly. Essentially, it means we can turn you into an expert assassin or a trained diplomat in a matter of moments. The only downside is the process can only be used once per year due to potential brain damage."

"Okay, so which do you plan to make me, an assassin or a diplomat?" Avala asked.

"I was thinking a special agent, capable of a mixture of tasks and trained in a variety of skills. Essentially, someone who can do anything we need them to do. Interested?"

"I . . . want to end Daigix. Then I will help," Avala replied quietly.

"Excellent. We have been meaning to force him out of that body for a while. We will get you through training, and then you and Agent Allan can take him out. Sound like a deal?"

Avala looked up and nodded.

Sylvia smiled. "Then come with me."

3

THE ILLUSION

Sylvia led Avala to a room with a strangely shaped table in the center. The table, or perhaps it was a bed, was padded with some soft material that she did not recognize. Sylvia helped her onto it and had her lie down. Suddenly, Avala was scared. What was going to happen to her?

Sylvia senses her panic. "No need to be afraid," she said softly. "This won't hurt, and it will be over before you know it. It works better if you're calm."

Avala tried to calm herself, with little success. Sylvia had another person put a metal hat on Avala's head. It also covered her face. A strange smell assaulted her. Yet, for some reason, instead of experiencing more fear, she began feeling calm.

A distant voice said something about beginning a process, but she could not quite make out what it said as the world around her went dark.

Avala opened her eyes. She was standing on a platform that was floating in a void. Stars and wisps of energy swirled in the distance.

"I've been waiting for you," a voice behind her said.

Avala spun around and saw a strange woman standing before her. She looked similar to Avala's kind, but instead of hair, strands of scales flowed from her head. Her eyes were wide, amber, and had slits for pupils, similar to Avala's but much larger.

"What are you?" Avala asked, noticing her voice echoed around her.

"I am Yasal, and I've been expecting you for a long time," the woman replied with a sad smile.

Avala tensed up in fear. How had Yasal found her here? For that matter, where was *here*? Why did she not remember how she got there?

"Where are we?" she asked quietly.

"This is the mindworld of the cast-offs, the one we all share. You are the first of your kind to come here, but I knew you would come."

Suddenly Avala remembered her brother's death, and she was filled with rage. "My brother was killed by your kind! Because of your stupid need for sacrifices!"

Yasal laughed. "Silly girl! He was not killed so much as absorbed. His life force was used to strengthen our portion of the mindworld. He is now a part of us. His memories and soul live on within us."

"No!" That was even worse. The thought of Vran being absorbed by these monsters enraged her. "You will release him! Now!"

"What good will that do? It won't bring him back from the—"

Yasal cut her words short when Avala launched herself at her. Avala clawed at Yasal, trying to hurt her in any way she could. Suddenly, a glint of light from inside Yasal's body caught Avala's attention. She did not know why, but it reminded her of Vran. She reached for it and somehow pulled it out of Yasal and into herself.

"Stupid girl! Get off me!" Yasal pushed her with such strength that Avala flew backward into the void.

Her back hit something hard. Her eyes flew open. She was once again in the room with the strange bed. The weird hat was off, and Sylvia was looking down at her.

"You're awake," Sylvia said casually.

Avala! Is that you? Vran's voice said in her mind. Her eyes went wide. Was she hearing ghosts?

Avala! It's me, Vran! You freed me from Yasal, remember?

Avala nodded, as if to answer. *Where are you?* she thought to herself, hoping Vran would hear.

I appear to be in some sort of strange floating ruins, but I can see you through a window of sorts. I . . . I think I may be in your mind, Vran said.

"Avala, are you okay?" Sylvia asked.

Avala nodded. She wasn't going to tell Sylvia about this. It would only make things weirder.

"We should test to see if the skill implant worked. Do you think you can get up now?"

"How long has it been?" Avala inquired.

"Six hours." Sylvia smiled at Avala's confused look. "That's the equivalent of about three of your bell tolls."

Avala nodded and slowly pushed herself up. She looked around. The room seemed different, but she couldn't place her finger on what it was. Perhaps she was just perceiving things differently.

"Come this way, please," Sylvia said.

Once again she led Avala through the winding halls and corridors. They stopped at a room that was empty except for large glowing pillars in each of the four corners. Sylvia put her hand on Avala's shoulder. "Good luck with the testing."

Sylvia left her standing there, confused. What was she supposed to do? As soon as she thought it, the room morphed into a large outdoor area. She was once again on her home world. She recognized the stars as that of mid-year. It must have been the month of the All Seer, because the constellation of Aravvatis, the All Seer, was clearly visible. That was odd, since she left during the month of the Great Sea.

Suddenly, a horn sounded. She recognized it as a hunter's horn. Before she could figure out where it came from, an arrow whizzed past her and hit a nearby tree. Instinct kicked in—instinct that she didn't know she had.

She dodged as an arrow whooshed right through where she had just been. She looked around for something to defend herself with. She found a Kyati sword sitting next to a tree. She grabbed it and held it out in front of her. She used the middle part of the blade, which was two hands wide, as a shield, blocking an arrow from hitting her square in the face.

She rushed forward, keeping low to the ground and ducking behind cover when needed. After a few moments, she saw her attacker. She was shocked to find it wasn't an Athakarin but a being similar to Yasal. It was a man though. Avala charged with her weapon raised, rage filling her. If this was the same type of being as those her people worshipped, it did not deserve to live.

She swung her blade at her opponent, only to be blocked by the blade of its Ijix bow. She leaped back a few paces and pretended to attack his side, then swung below his defenses at his legs. Her blade slashed through right above his knees, causing him to fall to the ground. She was about to finish the job when a voice rang through her thoughts. *We are better than our foes, because we show them mercy. To kill an enemy who cannot defend himself makes us as bad as them.*

She faltered. It was not Vran's voice but Commander Sylvia's. Was she in her head as well? Then she remembered that they had transferred skills and knowledge to her mind. This was most likely wisdom that the humans had placed in her mind to help her.

She sighed. The words rang true. She did not want to become like her enemy. She looked at the Yajiran. Something inside told her this was not a Yajixa, because he would have abandoned his body by now.

A sudden sound made her duck, right as another arrow flew above her. She turned and saw five Yajirans with arrows aimed at her. "Surrender now, rebel, and you may yet appease Yasal with your sacrifice."

She slowly lowered her weapon. Out of the corner of her eye, she spotted a strange device on the side of the downed Yajiran. She recognized it as something she could use. She grabbed it, pulled a pin out of the top, and threw it at her enemies. It exploded in a shower of fire and smoke. She turned and ran. If she followed the stars, she would be able to get to safety in the frozen wastes.

As she ran, she heard the Yajirans following. Somehow, they had survived. One of them blew a horn, and seven more came out from the trees in front of her. She charged straight at them and leaped at the front-most one. Her foot collided with his face, and she used that to propel herself over the others' heads.

She landed behind them and kept running, looking up to check the stars. The South Star was to her right, which meant she was heading the correct way. As she ran, the air began to chill around her, the ground covered in a thin layer of snow and ice.

The Yajirans were still on her trail. Arrows whizzed past her, but she kept running. Trees were becoming scarce, which was a sign she was approaching the frozen wastes of the east. A crevice came up in front of her. One of the rope bridges, erected by her people, was just ahead. She rushed across and found another sword stuck in the ice on the other side. She grabbed it and slashed the ropes of the bridge.

They would not be able to get her for a while. That would give her time to rest. She walked over to a large boulder and sat behind it. Suddenly, the world around her returned to the room with the four glowing pillars. The boulder disappeared a few moments later, confusing her.

Sylvia came up to her, slowly clapping her hands. "Very good! You did excellent!" She smiled at the confused look on Avala's face.

"That was all a clever illusion. You were in this room the entire time. You could call it human 'magic,' but we call it technology. The knowledge that was transferred to you came from several of our top agents on Evelon II. So, it's tailored to fit your planet and race. That hologram was a test to see if the knowledge transferred properly. You were never actually in danger."

Avala blushed in embarrassment. How could she have fallen for such an illusion? It had felt so real. "Now what?" she asked.

"Now you and Agent Allan will take on the mission of ending Daigix. After that, you will help us in our war, as per our deal. Now follow me. We need to get you equipped for the mission."

4

A NEW HOPE

Avala stood in the circular room with the plate on the floor. Alvaj stood beside her doing a final check of his equipment.

"The MELT transporter will place you down east of Childya, on the edge of the Frozen Wastes." Sylvia's voice came from all around them, as if emanating from the walls. "Ready?"

"I'm ready," Alvaj said, then turned to Avala. "How about you?"

She nodded. "Ready."

"Good luck."

With that, the world around her melted away, replaced with a frozen forest. Avala looked around. No one else in sight. That was a good thing. If others had seen them, their cover would have been blown.

"The town is this way," Alvaj said, already heading west.

Avala followed. In truth, she dreaded returning to her village. To blend in, she would once again have to submit herself to the oppression of men. However, she would make the one who killed her brother pay, and that was worth it.

As they walked, it became clear that someone was watching them. She looked at Alvaj, and he nodded, sensing it too. Moments later, a group of men came out from the trees. They had arrow aimed at them. More specifically, they had arrows aimed at her. She froze.

Alvaj took a few steps forward, turned to her, and then addressed the men. "That's her! The witch who consorted with the Devalra! I brought her to you, just as you asked." As he said it, Daigix stepped out from the shadows, smiling.

All Avala could do was look at Alvaj in shock. He was working for the Yajirans? That wasn't possible—unless this was all a bad dream. She shook herself, hoping to wake up, but it seemed this was real.

"Ah, Avala, ever since your husband informed us of your treachery, we have been looking all over for you. Now it seems our hunt is over. Come peacefully, and you may appease the spirits with your sacrifice."

"No! You Yajirans will not win! You're tyrants! My people will not be slaves to you any longer!" she yelled, pulling a throwing dagger from a band on her wrist. Before anyone could stop her, she hurled it at Daigix's heart. He dropped as it buried itself deep into his chest, orange blood oozing everywhere.

The others did not have time to react as Alvaj shot one it the face with a Vaix dart, its poison eating at his face. The rest reacted to the dual threats with utter panic. They fired their arrows, but Avala was already on the move.

She dodged three arrows, then pulled out her Vaix dart thrower, loading it with a dart. She twirled it above her head, launching the dart at a nearby enemy. It embedded itself in his chest, and the poison began eating his armor. He screamed as it ate through to the skin beneath.

Alvaj threw a dagger square in the face of one man. Then she rushed over to retrieve her own dagger, throwing it at another enemy. It pierced his throat with pinpoint accuracy.

The last remaining man backed away in terror. Avala was about to end him but realized that even if there were no witnesses, the

Yajixa inside Daigix would still be able to warn others about their betrayal. She let the man leave. Daigix had most likely escaped. He would awaken in an innocent Yajiran or Athakarin and take over that person's body.

She gave Alvaj a stern look. "Why? Why did you do it? You betrayed me and lured me into a trap!"

He shook his head, holding his hands behind his back, "It wasn't you I lured into a trap; it was them. I'm sorry I didn't tell you, but I wasn't sure you would have liked the idea. Besides, we couldn't have killed him in town; there would have been far too many guards."

"You broke my trust!" she yelled.

"Did you ever trust me?" he asked, his face expressionless. She said nothing. "I thought not. You don't trust men at all. Many women among your people don't either."

"What do we do now?" she asked. The snow on the ground was stained orange with blood. The sight of it almost made her vomit. She had done this. *They deserved it,* she told herself.

They were only doing as they were told, Vran's voice inside her said, *but they would have killed you without hesitation. So in a way, they did deserve it. But in another . . ..*

She nodded solemnly.

"We should signal for a pickup." Alvaj pulled out a little device and did something with it. "Due to safety mechanisms, they won't receive the message for a while. About one bell toll length. I'll explain why another time. We should find shelter."

She looked around. The trees were covered in ice, but they still had leaves. It was cold and dark in the east all year long. The trees survived on very little light, so their leaves were big and dark. Their only source of light was the moon, also known as the Crescent of Zayil, which was in the sky now.

She looked to the west. The edge of the horizon was gold with fire. It was always bright there. The land of Eternal Fire lay beyond the horizon. However, a ways before the horizon were the lights of her old village. They would find no refuge there. No doubt, everyone had heard of her witchcraft from Daigix before he set out on his hunt. Alvaj's plan literally left them out in the cold.

"There's a cave entrance nearby. We should head there," Alvaj said from behind her.

Avala knew the cave he was talking about. Everyone from her village avoided it. It was the home of a great and angry spirit beast, known as Avli. Apparently, Avli killed all but a rare few who entered her home. The ones she spared were said to be blessed by her. However, the priests always said the Majiril or Spirit Beasts were not true spirits like the Yaji and thus did not have the power to bless people.

"What about Avli?" she asked.

He looked at her and sighed. "I don't believe in ghosts or spirits. If Avli exists, she is most likely just an animal. Come, we'll deal with her when we get there."

After a quarter bell toll of walking, they reached the cave. As a child of six, she snuck away from home to look at the cave. Fear had paralyzed her when she heard something roar inside and saw glowing eyes within. Now it seemed quiet and empty.

Alvaj stepped inside, and Avala followed. Immediately after entering, the air warmed up. She looked around, allowing her eyes to adjust. The cave was large, with a pool in the center. On a small island within the pool was the skeleton of a large creature. It seemed ancient.

"See? It's already dead," Alvaj said. No sooner were the words out of his mouth than the bones started moving.

Avala watched in horror as the skeleton assembled itself. Within a few moments, the entire skeleton was complete, and its eye sockets started glowing. It stared at her and Alvaj hungrily and then roared.

To Avala's horror and confusion, Alvaj stepped toward it. "I am Agent Allan, code-name Alvaj. Entry code D four nine Y."

The monster's eyes turned green, and a woman's voice came out from its mouth. "Identity confirmed. Access code confirmed. Transferring you to Hideout Avli."

Moments later, the world around Avala melted away, and she found herself in another cave. The area in which she and Alvaj had appeared looked like a makeshift version of the MELT transporter room from the command center.

Alvaj turned to her and smiled. "See? What did I tell you? There's no such thing as ghosts."

Avala sighed. This was a hideout for human spies; that much was clear. She was kind of sad though, because that meant the stories of blessing were false. She smiled at herself. After everything she had seen, she had let herself be fooled by the illusion of a spirit beast. No doubt she still had a lot to learn.

"Halt right there, Yajixa scum!" a woman's voice said from across the small cave. A Yajiran woman stepped forward pointing a strange weapon straight at Avala's chest.

"Jira! What are you doing? Put the beam pistol down!" Alvaj scolded.

"You brought this Yajixa here? To destroy us?" the Yajiran asked angrily.

Alvaj looked at the Yajiran and then at Avala. "You're not a Yajixa, are you?"

"I don't think so. How would I be able to tell?" Avala asked innocently. She had a sudden fear that killing Daigix had placed the Yajixa inside her. Then she stopped herself. "Why is there a Yajiran here?"

"I am *not* a filthy Yajiran! I am a proud Athakri!" the woman said. "A Yajixa soul stealer like yourself should know that! I can see in your mind the souls you have fed on!"

Avala gasped. She suddenly understood. "Wait! You mean Vran? I didn't feed on him! He's my brother! I rescued him from Yasal in my dream!"

"From your dream?" Jira asked, slightly lowering her weapon.

"When they did the knowledge transfer, I dreamt I was in some sort of weird void. Yasal was there. And somehow I rescued my brother from her when I attacked her. When I woke up, he was in my head!"

Jira lowered her weapon further. "What about the others?"

"Others?" she asked, confused.

"We recently dispatched a group of Athakarins who attacked us. Maybe she absorbed them," Alvaj suggested.

"If this is true . . . it means . . . .." Jira looked at Avala with a hopeful expression. "We may finally have what we need to win this war!" She lowered her weapon and smiled. "Welcome to Hideout Avli. I'm Jira, leader of security for the Athakri here. You will prove invaluable to the war effort."

5
THE PROPHECY

"Why didn't you tell us when it happened?" Commander Sylvia asked in exasperation.

They were back at the command center. Alvaj said they were brought back in response to his message from one bell toll earlier. Avala didn't understand how it worked. However, she understood that Sylvia was upset at her.

"I thought you would think I was crazy," she replied, looking at her feet. She did not like being scolded. It reminded her too much of her past.

Sylvia took a deep breath. "Well, at least we know now. What's done is done. I should be glad we finally have a Yajixa on our side."

"How do you know I'm a Yajixa?" Avala asked. "I haven't changed bodies yet."

"I don't, but our Athakri friends do. That's good enough for me," Sylvia replied sternly. Then she sighed. "I guess it's not your fault. All this was new to you. I can't blame you for not trusting anyone after all you've been through."

Avala said nothing, just continued to look at her feet.

"We should talk to the Athakri," Sylvia continued. "They'll be able to tell us more about your potential abilities. I'll send a message asking for someone knowledgeable of such things to come join us here. You are dismissed." She paused when she noticed Avala's sullen expression. "I'm sorry I was so harsh on you. I guess I'm used to dealing with well-trained individuals. They would know better than to keep a secret from me. I should also remember that you are not actually under my command." She smiled. "Go on and do something fun."

Avala nodded and smiled back weakly. Then she left Sylvia's office and headed for the nearest Adjutant panel. "How do I get to the illusion room with the four pillars?" She did not know what it was called, but she wanted to see what else it could do.

The face appeared on the panel. "There are three holographic virtual reality platforms—HVRPs—in the complex. One of the HVRPs is for official business only, and the other two are for personal use."

"I want one that I can experiment in," she said hopefully.

"Given your credentials, HVRP B is both nearby and accessible by you. Follow the yellow lights through the complex, please."

With that, the floor lit up with a yellow line. Avala followed it, trying not to step off it, fearing that if she did, she would lose the line. While following it, she noticed that other lines of a multitude of colors lit up the floor when other people were nearby. She also noticed that most of the people weren't walking only on the lines. She blushed when she realized she had taken what the Adjutant had said far too literally. The rest of the way, she followed the yellow line but did not step on it.

When she finally reached her destination, the room looked just like what she remembered of the other one, except it had an Adjutant panel just inside the door. It must have noticed her, because it lit up when she entered. "Greetings. Please state the nature of hologram you wish to experience today."

Avala thought for a moment. There were places on her world that she had never seen but wanted to visit, such as Avraintix, the City of the Fire, on the edge of the Eternal Fire. Or the City of Trees in the Northlands, the real name of which was a secret. Or perhaps Ecrekio, the City of Bones, an ancient ruin, graveyard, and city, all built underground. But what about places not on her world? She knew nothing of them. Maybe she would ask about them at some point. For the moment, she wanted to experience the one nearest her old home. "Ecrekio, the City of Bones, please," she replied.

"Please, choose the responses for the following settings," the Adjutant said. "Realistic dangers? Yes or no?"

"No," she answered; she just wanted to explore.

"Confirmed. Use actual location scan? Yes or no?"

"What does that mean?" Avala asked.

"If 'yes,' then the system will do a detailed scan of the region over several minutes, attempting to create the most accurate and up-to-date hologram of the area. This is only possible for real locations. If 'no' is selected, the system will use the most recent version of the area."

"I guess, yes." She did not understand what a minute was, but if it was a measurement of time, it couldn't be too long, could it?

"Confirmed. Use accurate simulated people and creatures or use custom people and creatures?"

"Accurate," she replied. She wanted it to be like the real thing.

"Confirmed. Processing data. Please stand by."

Moments later the room shifted into a large space. In front of her was the cave entrance to Ecrekio. The massive archway made of crystal, stone, and bones stood several times her height. Two guards, wearing armor made of skulls and bones stood on either side. They nodded at her. A sudden fear overwhelmed her that these people knew who she was, that she was a rebel. Then she remembered it was an illusion, that the people weren't real. She walked forward, and they let her pass.

Once inside she followed the massive winding staircase down into the depths of the mountains. The walls were lined with countless statues of her people's great heroes. She followed the staircase down for a ways before it split into ten separate pathways. She chose one at random and started down it.

The tunnel was lit with torches that seemed to burn without fuel. The walls were lined with hollows holding stone boxes, shaped and decorated like people. On shelves below the people were small trinkets and treasures, such as birth rings and necklaces. Further on the tunnel opened into a massive room filled with rows of stone walls—each one an adult's height—decorated with murals and writing.

She had heard about the Walls of Prophecy before. They were scattered throughout the City of Bones. It was said that the city predated the birth of her people, and the spirits had found it when they claimed the world. If her recent knowledge of her world proved true, that meant it was either made by the humans or was there before them.

She walked among the rows of walls, not understanding most of the writing. "I wonder what they say," she said aloud to herself.

The Adjutant panel appeared behind her, startling her. "Translation in progress. The text appears to be from the Echarikith, a race that inhabited most of the galaxy three million years ago. Translations are appearing now. Note that they are, at best, eighty percent accurate." The panel disappeared again, merging back into the illusion.

Text in her people's language started to appear above the strange writing. She was never fully taught to read, so she did not understand many of the words, but the Adjutant was able to help her in those cases.

After several bell tolls had passed, she came across a wall that stood out from the rest, not because the style was different but because it was unmistakably about her! Her birth rings were clearly visible along the top. A girl bearing her face was in the center, and her name was written clearly on the wall. The writing read, "We see the girl Avala. We see she will awaken us, after we fall. We see she is a half-breed. We see that she takes part in a war. We see that she becomes a shifter of bodies. We see that she becomes a collector of souls. We see the girl Avala. We see that she will awaken us, after we fall."

She couldn't believe her eyes. "Is this actually in the real place?" she asked the Adjutant.

"All details have been collected from the most recent MELT scans. Everything you see is as accurate as if you were in the actual location."

She needed to show it to Commander Sylvia. "Is it possible to ask Commander Sylvia to come here?"

"Attempting to contact Commander Sylvia M." The Adjutant paused. "Contact established."

"You wanted something, dear?" Sylvia's voice said from the panel.

"I found something in an illusion of the City of Bones. I think you should see it. I'm not going to keep a secret from you this time."

"I understand," Sylvia replied. "I'll be there soon."

After an agonizing wait, a door materialized in the prophecy wall behind Avala, and Commander Sylvia walked through it. Then the door vanished. "What did you want to show me?"

Avala pointed at the wall. Sylvia looked at it and nodded. "Adjutant, please translate into English and Athakarin."

Moments later, two versions of the text were visible along with the original, one Avala could sort of read and one she could not.

Sylvia gasped. "I have heard about the Echarikith ruins on Evelon II and how the Echarikith had ways of seeing the future, but I didn't believe it was this accurate. Those are your birth rings, correct?"

Avala nodded.

"Fascinating. I'll admit, if you had tried telling me this without showing me, I wouldn't have believed you." She paused. "Adjutant, image and translate all the prophecy walls in the City of Bones, then send them to the information-processing teams. Also, send a copy to my office." After the Adjutant acknowledged the request, Sylvia turned to Avala and smiled. "It seems you are destined for greatness, child. We are going to see what else we can learn from these ruins. Maybe we'll discover things that will help us in our war."

Avala smiled. She hoped she was actually that special. It would make up for all the bad things in her past.

6

THE MINDSCAPE

Avala had returned to her quarters and was just finishing eating before sleep. The Athakri had sent one of their brightest to the command center. However, by the time he and his guard arrived, Avala was too hungry and tired to continue.

She was preparing to go to sleep. Normally, she would have prayed to the spirits, as was tradition, but after all the recent events, she no longer felt it was necessary. She had the Adjutant light the hearth. Then, remembering the privacy setting, pressed the blue button. She stripped out of her dirty clothes and donned a simple robe that she had the Adjutant make for her, using its strange magic.

Lying down among the pillows by the hearth, she listened to the sound of the fire. It might have been an illusion, but it sounded real. The noises from "outside" the window almost made her forget that she was not in the world where she grew up on. Finally, she drifted off to sleep.

She opened her eyes. She was standing in an ancient ruin. The strange thing was, everywhere she looked, rocks and plant life were floating in the air. She saw the sky, or what passed for the sky, through massive cracks in the structure. It was a dark and nearly empty void with wisps of energy floating through it.

Through a doorway, she heard angry shouting. When she peeked through, chills traveled down her spine. Nearly half a dozen men stood around someone lying on the ground, bloody and beaten. It was her brother, Vran.

She looked around for a weapon but found she was still wearing her sleeping gown. Without a thought, she waved both hands in front of her chest in a downward arc, first toward each other, then away. As she did, her clothing changed to rugged leather armor. Her feet were still bare, so she stomped them, causing leather boots to appear. Making the motion of drawing a weapon from her side, she was surprised to find a sword in her hand. She did not know how she did any of it; it just happened, like magic.

She pushed through the doorway and shouted a battle cry. All the men turned and looked at her in terror. She stopped cold. She recognized them. They were the ones who she and Alvaj had killed. All of them were there except for Daïgix. Many of them fell to their knees, begging for mercy. Looking at each one in turn, she imagined them in chains. Before her eyes, each of them was suddenly chained to a nearby wall.

Then she looked at her brother. He appeared badly burned and was beaten, broken, and almost dead. Beginning to cry, she realized what she had to do. Calming her thoughts, she pictured him alive and well, like he used to be—strong, brave, handsome, and kind. Before her eyes, his wounds healed, and life returned to his body. He stood up.

Upon seeing her, he smiled. "Avala, it seems you've found a way to visit your own mind."

She was shocked. Was that why these strange things were happening? "This isn't a dream? This is my mind?"

"I believe so." He looked around, pointing out various features around them. "These ruins appear to be of similar design to the temple at our old home. There are also parts of the other structures visible there, though why they all appear to be in ruins remains to be seen."

Avala saw what he meant. Everything floating in the void appeared to be from her memories.

He looked at her. "I'm proud of you. I witnessed most of what has happened to you since you rescued me. You have proven what I have always thought—that women are capable of being more than just possessions."

"You thought that?" she asked, touched that he had believed it.

"Indeed. However, it must have been that way of thinking that got me sacrificed." He sighed, "How about while you're here I show you around? Before those thugs showed up, I had some time to find some interesting things."

He led her through the maze of ruins. Some parts reminded her of the human complex. Other places reminded her of the City of Bones. Everywhere she went, she saw things from her memories, scenes from her past re-enacted by ghostly figures. He showed her the various windows into reality, where she saw her sleeping body. There were also doors of various designs, each of which she had seen before in reality and all of which were locked from the other side. The sounds coming from them suggested massive numbers of people were behind them.

They stopped at a door that was decorated with bones and skulls. However, unlike the other doors, she had never seen one like it. What was it doing there? She gave Vran a questioning look.

He shrugged. "I haven't gone through it. It looks dangerous. Maybe you'd like to look. You can handle it more than me. Look at how you dealt with those goons."

She decided to open it. Inside was a massive chamber. Its walls were decorated with the mural from the prophecy wall about her, repeated over and over. A large statue of a skeletal figure was in the center. She stepped closer. The statue moved and looked directly at her. She froze.

"We see the girl, Avala," it said in a thundering voice. "We see her come to us. We see her awaken us. We see her . . . free us?"

She was unsure how to respond. The creature was using the same type of phrasing as the Walls of Prophecy. Could it be the one who wrote them? How did it come to be in her mind?

"What are you?" she asked.

"We are the ones who came before. We are the ones who saw what was to come. We are the ones who ruled all worlds with life. We are the Echarikith."

Avala looked at it, confused. Why did it keep saying "we"? Was it really multiple creatures speaking at once?

"Why are you here?"

"We see our home. We see the multitude of drones. We see a space rock plunge toward the core. We feel the ground shake. We feel our world break. We scream in fear. We see the drones on other worlds. We see them break free from us. We are imprisoned. We are enslaved."

That raised more questions than answers. "What will happen if I free you?" Avala knew the answer would be even more confusing, but she couldn't just free the thing without asking about the consequences.

"We will be grateful. We will make new drones. We will once again bring harmony. We will once again create life. We will once again live in reality."

Something about what it said scared her. She couldn't place her finger on it though. She shook her head; no being deserved to be trapped or enslaved. She would free it. She imagined a doorway big enough for the creature in the far wall. She pictured it opening and the creature walking free into the void.

Before her eyes, things played out as she imagined. Suddenly, she felt like the world around her was being ripped apart, like she was being ripped apart.

Her eyes flew open. Once again she was in her quarters. Her entire body screamed with pain. It didn't hurt the last time she woke up from the mindworld. What was going on? She sat up, only to look directly into the eyes of a young Yajiran girl. She nearly screamed. "What are you doing in here?"

The girl giggled. "You freed me, remember?" Then she frowned. "Or do you not remember? I probably looked a lot bigger and more skeletal. I think I was in your mind, perhaps. Don't you remember?"

Avala frowned. This was the creature she had freed? It was just a young girl! "What are you?" she asked.

"I am one of the Echarikith Mind Prophets. My name is Echniath, I think. It's been too long."

"What were you doing in my mind?" Avala asked, still confused.

"The Yajirans imprisoned us in the mindworld long ago. The strongest of them stole us from our bodies and used our powers for their own ends. I don't know how I ended up in your mind, but I've passed through quite a few over the years. This body is similar to the one I had before my spirit was stolen from it."

"You're just a child though," Avala replied.

"Well, yes and no. This body may be that of a child—like my previous three—but I have lived in countless bodies before. As a member of the Echarikith consciousness, I can create a new body for myself when this one dies."

"You're a Yajixa!" Avala cried.

Echniath shook her head. "No. The Yajixa are descendants of cast-off bodies of our spirits. The Yajirans, as they call themselves, were once the bodies of our drones—the individual spirits of the Echarikith consciousness. When our core fell, we were knocked out of our bodies temporarily, and new life and thought flowed into them and other newly born races.

"We allowed them to go free, not wishing to enslave them. So, we created new bodies for ourselves. Eventually, the Yajirans realized our power and stole our spirits, all in one strike. The original ten, who devised the plot to steal and enslave us, became the first Yajixa. Some of their descendants were born as new Yajixa, though they still devised ways of making more. It was because of our enslavement that they have their powers."

"So, I no longer have any powers?" Avala asked. She had come to that conclusion due to the fact that Echniath was in front of her and, therefore, not in her mind.

"In gratitude, I left part of myself in your mind. You will still have the power. You'll need it to help defeat the Yajixa and free my kin. The Yajixa have been careful to indoctrinate every new Yajixa into their beliefs. But I saw long ago that you would escape them."

All this seemed strange to Avala. How was any of this possible? Was it just a dream? "Sylvia will want to talk to you," she said finally.

7

THE LR-VRP

"So, you're telling me that the Yajixa get their power by enslaving members of your race in their minds?" Commander Sylvia asked, looking at the young Yajiran girl in disbelief.

Avala did not blame her. It was hard to trust a child with such outlandish stories, since children were so prone to make-believe. Even so, she knew Echniath was telling the truth.

"When I woke up from freeing the being in my mind, she was right there. She also was able to tell me what I saw in my mind," Avala said.

"You already said that," Sylvia replied. "Remember that the Yajirans share a connected mind with you; she most likely just spied on you."

Avala hadn't considered that possibility. However, some part of her felt this was no hoax.

"I'm telling the truth!" Echniath said firmly.

As she said it, the door opened, and the two Athakri who had previously come to the base entered. Avala recognized one of them as Jira, who she had met briefly in the cave of the spirit beast.

"Greetings, Avala. Did you sleep well? I . . .." Jira broke off as she looked at the child. With trembling hands, she pulled out her weapon at pointed it at the girl.

The other Athakri, a man, stumbled back. "Powerful ones protect us," he said under his breath.

"What is up with you two?" Sylvia asked, "I will not have you pointing weapons at—"

Before she could finish, Jira fired. A beam of light shot toward the girl. It was stopped by an invisible barrier just short of the child. The smell of smoke filled the air. Jira's eyes widened even farther when she saw her target was unharmed.

"What was the meaning of that?" Sylvia yelled.

Jira did not seem to hear her. "She can't be one of the Ancients. The Yajixa destroyed them all." She lowered her weapon slowly, still shaking.

Echniath spoke, but her voice was like the creature's in Avala's mind. "We saw them come. We saw them aim. We saw them shoot. We protected our drone. We saw them bow. The prophecy is fulfilled."

Avala was confused by the "bow" part until she noticed that the Athakri were already beginning to get on their knees. "The Ancients have returned to us," the male Athakri said, though something seemed odd about it.

Sylvia looked shocked. "I guess that solves the question of whether you're telling the truth," she said softly.

"Please, there is no need for worship," Echniath cried. "I only seek the return of my kin."

The two Athakri rose slowly. They avoided looking at the child, as if afraid to meet her gaze. "How did you return to us, Ancient One, after the Yajixa destroyed your kind?" Jira asked reverently.

"The Yajixa stole us from our bodies; they did not destroy us. Have the Athakri truly lost so much of their history?" the young girl replied sadly.

"I don't want to interrupt, but what exactly do you mean by 'their history'?" Sylvia asked. "As far as I'm aware, the Athakri weren't around as long ago as the fall of the Echarikith, yet you're implying its part of their history?"

The two Athakri and Echniath looked at Sylvia as if she had just insulted them. "We Athakri are descendants of the final bodies of the Echarikith. Many eventually joined the Yajirans and sullied their blood with those traitors. We few who did not have been hiding for millions of years. Countless generations remained hidden from the Yajixa until about two thousand years ago, when *your* kind led them right to us!" Jira said bitterly.

"Our ancestors didn't realize the Yajirans were any different from your kind!" Sylvia growled. "Besides, Avala's people are proof that your ancestors and mine seemed to get along well enough!"

"Please, don't fight!" Avala cried. Everyone turned to her, and she blushed in embarrassment, but she continued anyway. "Why are you fighting over something that happened before any of us were born? The Yajirans see us all as enemies! Fighting doesn't help anyone."

"She has a point," Echniath said in a singsong voice.

Commander Sylvia sighed, and the two Athakri stood down. "You're right. We aren't enemies. Acting like such will only lead to more problems." Sylvia lowered her head. "I apologize for my ignorance. Though the Athakri have never been open to sharing their history, I should have made an effort to learn what I could before commenting."

After a long period of silence, Jira nodded. "Let's get to what we came for. We're here to assess Avala's abilities." She motioned toward the other Athakri. "This is Orrain. He is the most knowledgeable among us on matters involving the Yajixa."

Orrain bowed his head. "It's an honor to meet you, Avala. The first Athakarin to become a Yajixa, and the first to escape their grasp—you will be most welcome in our fight. I hope I can train you well,"

"Hi, I guess," was all Avala could say.

"If I may, I would like to help train her," Echniath said excitedly. "My insight might be useful." It seemed that sometimes she acted like a mere child while other times she seemed ancient and wise; this was the former.

"As you wish, Ancient One." Orrain turned to Avala. "We should go somewhere quieter and with lots of space." He looked at Sylvia. "One of your HVRPs might be what we need, but it would be better if we could use Project LR-VRP."

Sylvia was silent for a moment, then nodded. "Right this way." Instead of leaving her office, she walked to the far wall. She touched it in a strange pattern, and the wall melted away, revealing a door. "In here." She opened the door, revealing a massive space filled with plants of all shapes and sizes. "Please, be careful," she said solemnly. Avala, Echniath, and the two Athakri entered the doorway, the door closing behind them.

The place was amazing. Avala had never seen so many large plants. It seemed more alien to her than anything she had seen so far. Far above her, through the canopy, was a metal ceiling. The walls were also made of large metal plates, but she could only see the one the door was in.

"This is an advanced version of the HVRPs. Instead of holograms, they use actual objects made by turning energy into matter. It is so advanced that it can even create life, which the matter replicators can't do. For moral reasons, it is kept secret. Only those in command positions in the Republic of Earth know of their existence. And even then, they are expected to use the ability to create life only when absolutely necessary, plants excluded." Orrain started walking into the forest.

"How does it create life?" Avala asked.

"The technology of my people," Echniath responded quietly. "I would recognize it anywhere."

"That is correct, Ancient One," Orrain said. "The humans' allies among the Egrogans were the first ones to reverse engineer it, long before they became a space-faring civilization. However, they kept it a secret, due to implications on sapient and animal rights. Ninety years ago, the Egrogans and the humans agreed to combine the advanced technologies of the HVRPs and the life-shaping technologies. The original purpose was to create a space where scientists could experiment with various life forms to solve problems such as disease, starvation, and mental illness."

"If that's the case, why do only certain people know about it?" Jira asked.

"Excellent question. The simple answer is politics. The Republic's leadership changed shortly before the technology was completed. The new leadership did not approve of it and outlawed the technology. However, after the most recent election, the technology was once again allowed, but limits on who could use it were put in place to prevent abuse. Essentially, each leader of every high-tech military or science base has permission to use it and to allow others they deem responsible to use it."

"How do you know so much about it?" Avala asked. Orrain certainly seemed to know a great deal for it being such a secret.

"I have access to one myself, which was secretly installed in our hideout. The Republic gave it to the leader of our enclave as a token of goodwill. She, in turn, gave me access, due to my skills as a scientist and scholar," Orrain replied, smiling.

Finally, they came to a stop at a clearing in the forest. Orrain turned to Avala and smiled. "Now, Avala, as you no doubt know, any creature that dies near you has their life force—or soul, as some call it—absorbed into your mind."

Avala nodded. While inside her mind, she had encountered the men that she and Alvaj had killed, though the idea scared her.

"What you most likely did not know is that every creature you absorb can aid your mind in its functioning or increase your power," he continued. "Let me ask, have you traveled to your individual mindscape yet?"

Avala nodded. She did not know how she did it, but she had been inside her mind.

"Then you most likely saw that it was filled with ruins of structures that you have seen in your past, correct?"

She nodded again. What was he getting at?

"For you to function at your best, those structures must be repaired. Now, you can do this by entering your mind and willing them to be repaired, but they will need constant repair and thus limit what you will be able to achieve while in there. Alternatively, you can absorb creatures that have the knowledge to repair various structures and maintain them."

Avala did not like where this was going. He was going to use the room to create life that could repair structures, then execute them. That made her sick; she did not like the idea of killing innocent people. She was about to turn and walk away when Orrain noticed her sickened look. "Don't worry. We're not going to make sapient beings. Animals with the knowledge and instinct to repair structures will work just fine. Also, they won't feel anything when they die. We're not going to use conventional means of killing them."

She still didn't feel any better about it, but there was little she could do. She resigned herself to what was going to happen but made a mental note to tell Sylvia about it later.

"Adjutant," Orrain began, "create new life. Animal, based on Earth's monkey. No sapience. Limit self-awareness to minimum. Add knowledge about constructing and repairing all kinds of structures. Add instinct and the desire to repair and maintain structures. Add knowledge on how to use tools. Create twenty nearby. Confirm."

"Processing," the Adjutant said, her voice seeming to come from all around them. "Confirmed."

Suddenly, a group strange creatures appeared around them. They immediately started picking up sticks and leaves and putting them together as if trying to build.

"Adjutant," Orrain said, "kill last-created group of life. Modifiers: instant, painless, and humane."

Avala was in tears as the creatures suddenly fell limp. However, she felt a cold breeze coming from them directly toward her. She closed her eyes. If she listened hard enough she could hear them making their strange sounds inside her mind. She was sad for the loss of life, but her mind offered a place for them to live on. She attempted to find solace in that.

"Shall we continue?" Orrain asked, smiling.

Avala gave him a fearful look. What was wrong with him, that he could so casually do this? She was afraid he couldn't be trusted. She recognized that smile. Daigix had worn it many times after a sacrifice.

8

THE FIRST
TO FALL

Avala looked at Orrain, nodding more to herself than to him. She took a deep breath. "Let me try something."

He gestured for her to continue.

"Adjutant, knock out Orrain," she said before he could stop her.

"Confirmed," the Adjutant replied as Orrain fell unconscious, accompanied by a zapping sound.

Jira screamed and pointed her weapon at Avala. "You better have a good explanation for this!"

"He is a Yajixa," Echniath said before Avala could respond.

Jira blinked, then slowly looked down at Orrain. Her eyes went wide in horror as some power within her noticed what he was. "Adjutant," she said, "place Orrain in a containment field, and prevent him from using commands. Also, please alert Commander Sylvia that Orrain has been compromised by the Yajixa."

"Confirmed." A wall of purple light surrounded Orrain.

Echniath turned to Avala, "Now is your chance to fight the Yajixa. Let me help." She raised her hands above her head, and her

49

eyes began to glow blue. When she spoke again, her voice was that of the ancient being from Avala's mind. "We rip the Yajixa from its body. We throw him into our old prison. We send Avala in to fight it. We send Avala in to free our kin."

With those words, Avala fell to the ground as darkness enveloped her.

Avala opened her eyes to someone shaking her. It was Vran. She smiled, then she saw the look on his face. He was afraid of something.

"Avala! You're awake! The prison that held that being, it's been filled with something else, something that's breaking out! We have to stop it!"

She stood up and looked at what she was wearing. It was her clothes from reality. She knew they would not be enough. She performed the ritual that she had done before, and her clothing became thick leather armor. She pulled out her weapon and looked around at the changes since the last time she had been there. The "monkeys" that she had absorbed were doing everything they could to repair the structures, but it was slow work.

The world around her shook, and a roar sounded throughout the ruins. It was coming from the chamber from which she had freed Echniath. She knew she did not have enough power to defeat what was in there. She looked around for anything that she could use to her advantage.

Avala shook her head, remembering she was in charge there; that would be enough. She headed toward the chamber, with Vran behind her. When they arrived, they found the door badly dented; something was definitely trying to escape.

She looked at Vran, who nodded. She willed the door to open, and it did. Inside was a creature so hideous that she nearly screamed in fright. It appeared to be Yajiran, but it was a withered husk, near skeletal, though definitely alive. Countless blisters covered it, and worm-like things writhed throughout its body, coming out from what passed as flesh.

It charged her and impaled itself on her sword. She felt relieved that she had ended it so quickly. However, the creature was still very much alive. It ripped at her, tearing at her face with its skeletal hands. Vran launched himself at it, fighting with everything he had, but it remained focused on her, madly ripping and tearing. No matter what she did, she could not get it off.

She attempted to will the creature into a cage, but nothing happened. She pictured it dead and lifeless, but her will was not made a reality. She tried to push it off, but it was too strong.

She screamed as it tore into her eyes. The pain burned more than anything she had felt before. The more she struggled, the more the ruins around her collapsed. The creature tore into her chest, reaching for her heart.

She screamed in anger, fear, and hatred. The creature was trying to kill her inside her own mind! Suddenly, the world filled with fire. A spike came out of her hand and impaled the creature's face. All around her, metal spikes grew out of the walls. Fire and lava filled the area. She pushed the creature off her. She felt bigger, stronger, angrier.

The creature looked at her in fear, and she glared back with hatred. She reached into its chest and tore out what should have been its heart. Instead, she pulled out a ball of light. As she did, the creature went limp and started to dissolve.

As she calmed down, so did the world around her. She looked at the ball of light with awe. She knew what she needed to do. She willed an opening in the void and threw the ball of light into it. However, she did not wake up.

She turned to where the creature once lay, only to discover the body had been replaced with a door in the floor. She reached for it. Beyond the door she sensed countless souls trapped in fear and oppression. She paused, then opened it. The structures around her shifted and morphed. The doorway moved up to the wall. Beyond it she saw another mindscape, one with magnificent architecture, finely crafted and unlike the ruins on her side.

She also saw a multitude of people chained and forced to toil without rest for the mindscape's previous owner. Now that it belonged to her, she would not let them continue to be slaves. With a thought, she freed them all and let them know that she had killed their old master. She felt a warmth of gratitude and hope flow through her.

She looked around. That section of her mind needed work. She transferred the idea to the newly freed souls, requesting aid if they chose to give it. Many of the people and creatures within came forward while others stayed. She willed the doorway to widen until it was wide enough to let many through it.

Countless people came and thanked her, vowing their service to her. She smiled and told them to do what they desired, to make her mind a better place, to make it a home for themselves. She would not let her mind be shaped by her will alone. Everyone within deserved a chance to add something of their own, to carve out a place for themselves, to make it their home.

She remembered the men who she had chained up the previous time she was there. With another thought, she freed them and let them know she would allow them to do as they wished, as long as they did no harm.

A Yajiran man approached her. Some part of her recognized him. He bowed. "So it seems you have bested me and stolen my powers. I admit I am impressed."

Avala realized he was a remnant of the Yajixa she had defeated. "Why are you still here?" she asked.

"My name is Yvan. I am—was—one of the five Yajixa generals on Evelon II. But I was but a slave myself, you see. The Counsel of Ten enslaves every new Yajixa. Unfortunately, the only escape was the destruction of our power and the release of the Echarikith within us. By doing that, you have freed me. But alas, I now lack any power in the mindscape. All I can do now is try to survive."

"You aren't going to try to kill me again?" Avala asked suspiciously.

"How would I? None of the souls inside a mindscape can die, and only a Yajixa can kill another Yajixa. You have also made countless friends who would defend you from anything I could do. I am just one more soul who has been absorbed by your mind."

She could tell his words were true. He was no longer a Yajixa. She nodded at him. Suddenly, she felt as if she was being crushed by a tremendous weight.

Her eyes flew open. She looked around. She was on a soft bed in a room with white everywhere. Echniath, Jira, Orrain, Alvaj, and Commander Sylvia stood a distance away, talking quietly. She sat up. Echniath looked at her and smiled, giggling about something. Sylvia and Alvaj noticed and rushed over to her.

"You're awake, at last!" Sylvia said, sounding relieved.

Avala tried to speak, but her mouth was far too dry.

Alvaj reached over to a small table and grabbed a cup, handing it to her. "You seem thirsty, here."

Avala drank the cool water. She felt as if she had not had anything to drink in years. After finishing it, she set it back on the table. "How long have I been out?"

The two of them looked at each other, then back at her. "Nearly a year," Sylvia replied.

Avala looked at them in shock. It seemed like she had been inside her mind for less than a few bell tolls. Had she really been out that long?

Sylvia laughed. "Sorry, it was Echniath's idea to tell you that. It's only been a day."

The term seemed foreign to her, but some part of her mind informed her of the meaning. She smiled and looked past them at Orrain. "Wasn't he . . .." She did not know how to say it.

"Something that girl did restored him to himself," Sylvia said. "She claims you destroyed the Yajixa inside him. Also, it seems we have another Echarikith in the world, thanks to you."

Avala watched as a human-looking girl, about the same age as Echniath, entered the room and hugged the other girl, saying something to her.

"I don't know why such ancient beings keep making childlike bodies for themselves, but it seems to be a recurring theme," Alvaj said, chuckling.

Avala smiled. She felt more alive than ever. A great warmth welled up inside her. She felt she had the power to save her people at last. "We have work to do," she said with newfound confidence.

PART 2

-ECREKIO-

9

THE FIRST STRIKE

Avala looked through a pair of electronic binoculars. She saw the massive arched entrance to Ecrekio, the City of Bones. It had been only a few human months since she defeated her first Yajixa, Yvan. They had since made plans to take the City of Bones, due to its strategic location. It was only a few hundred kilometers south from Childya and Avli Hideout.

They had transformed Avli from a small Athakri hideout into a fully functional staging point, called Evelon II Planetary Command. Through some effort, they had connected it via an automated MELT transporter tunnel to the Republic Intelligence Command Center at Hydra Three as well as three other locations: the Republic Military command center, the Egrogan Military Science Headquarters, and the Nerafin Military Resource Center. That allowed them to funnel supplies and troops into the caves. They also expanded the caves, drilling new tunnels and entrances.

Spies from the Republic had infiltrated various major nations of the world, including the City of Bones, giving them a constant feed of intelligence. Some of the most recent intelligence had been that a minor nobleman, thought to be a minor Yajixa, was heading to

Ecrekio to mourn the passing of Daigix. The noble was supposed to be arriving any time. Once he was inside, they would strike.

"I think I see him," Alvaj said from beside her.

Avala checked her binoculars. It was definitely him. She saw a progression of servants riding Wrakta beasts, followed by a richly decorated cart bearing the symbols of Yasal. The progression stopped at the gate. They left their beasts of burden outside and proceeded into the city, carrying the nobleman on a covered platform.

Alvaj activated a small device in his hand. "The Lion has entered the cave. I repeat, the Lion has entered the cave."

Avala giggled at the phrasing. She would never get used to the strange code phrases that the intelligence agency used. He glared at her to be quiet, but she just smiled innocently at him.

They waited a while to ensure the potential Yajixa was far enough inside the city. Once they were certain enough time had passed, they hid their advanced technologies in their packs and left their hiding spot.

They headed toward the gate at a good pace. When they arrived, the guards stopped them. Avala saw a board beside the gate with various sheets of parchment on it. Two of them were wanted posters, one for her and one for Alvaj.

The lead guard glared at them, "Well, look what showed up on our doorstep. The witch and the terrorist. We're going to be rich."

Alvaj put on a look of confusion so realistic that it nearly fooled Avala. "I'm sorry, but what did you call us? My sister and I have come from the village of Dyak to the south. We are here to pay our respects to the recently departed priest of Childya. We give praise to the spirits every time the moon rises and every time it sets. We are neither witches nor terrorists."

He seemed so sincere that the guards were taken aback. However, one of them still seemed suspicious. "Why are people from the south paying respects to some random priest from a backwater town like Childya?"

Alvaj was prepared for that. "A few years back, we were traveling through Childya when our Wrakta beast took ill and could go no farther. Daigix was kind enough to sacrifice a young girl for us, so the spirits would heal our Wrakta. If not for him, we would have not been able to continue on our journey. We owe him our gratitude."

Avala paid special note of the guards, who looked faint when Alvaj mentioned the part about sacrificing the young girl. That indicated they might be willing to part from the ways of her people.

The lead guard sighed. "Your story seems believable enough. And I suppose you only vaguely look like the criminals in the posters. You may pass. May the spirits watch over you," he added as they passed.

Once inside, they proceeded down the winding staircase. Their entrance was a distraction to mask the approach of soldiers armed with tranquilizer guns. They would secure the entrance in a few moments.

Behind them, they heard the thump of bodies dropping to the ground. Moments later, a dozen heavily armed soldiers came down the staircase.

Alvaj took the communication device from his bag. "The hunters have entered the cave."

Avala could not help but giggle at the way he said it. He glared at her but stayed silent.

They continued down the stairs. Along the way, they equipped themselves with their gadgets and gear, no longer hiding their advanced technology.

At the bottom of the stairs, where it split off in ten directions, they took the least-traveled path, which was filled with dust. Intelligence reports suggested it had been taken over by large Drilik spiders, which the locals were afraid of messing with.

A while later, the passage became filled with giant nearly transparent webs. The ever-burning torches were extinguished there, making it obvious they were in the right area.

Avala and Alvaj equipped their rebreathers as she took a small canister from her bag. She pulled a pin from the top of the canister and threw it at the webbing. It pushed through, landing on the floor beyond. As it landed, it pumped out green gas.

Shrieking sounds came from farther in. Suddenly, a massive ten-legged creature burst out from the webs. The soldiers behind them fired a spray of tranquilizer rounds at it. The spider collapsed into a heap of limbs. Avala had been expecting it, but she was still startled.

Ahead of them, the gas from the canister started reacting with the webbing, igniting a fire. The webs were burning as far down the tunnel as they saw. They heard shrieking, followed by a wave of cold air. The spider caught fire as well and awoke shrieking in agony as the fire burned it to ashes.

Avala felt a tingling in her mind as the spiders started waking up within her mindscape. She used her thoughts to calm them, directing them to an unused corner of her mind, where they could build their nests and webs. She was saddened by yet another loss of life but knew it was for the greater good.

Once the fire died down, they continued on. The ever-burning torches had relit themselves, thanks to the fire, thus the path was visible before them. They continued to another massive chamber filled with countless Walls of Prophecy. Charred remains of spiders littered the area, showing just how effective the gas had been.

Alvaj pulled a head-sized device from his bag and set it down on the floor. He pressed several buttons, activating it. It would act as a beacon, allowing more people to be transported in and out by the staging point. The soldiers who had followed them took up positions around the room, guarding the beacon from potential threats.

Moments later the floor in front of them melted, and a strange display flowed upwards into the shape of two small figures. Then the floor flowed off the figures, revealing two young girls, one Yajiran and the other human-like. The Yajiran was Echniath, and the human-like one was the Echarikith drone that she had rescued from the Yajixa, Yvan. She called herself Elizba.

Apparently, the two Echarikith knew each other well. In the past, they had been lovers, but things had changed when they adopted new bodies. Back then, Echniath's body was male, but when he decided his next drone would be female, Elizba did not want to continue the relationship. The Echarikith had nothing against changing genders from body to body, neither did they have any problem with same-sex relationships, but some of them chose not to participate in such behavior.

The two girls bowed to them. Echniath smiled. "We have arrived to provide aid. Sylvia insisted we didn't come, but we came anyways."

"She was probably right not to want you to come. This is no place for little girls," Alvaj said sternly.

"We are *not* little girls! It's only these bodies that are young! We are both ancient," Elizba said, pouting.

Sometimes Avala found it hard to remember they were actually ancient beings, given that they liked to act like children rather than adults. Maybe that was why they chose to inhabit children's bodies, because they felt more like children.

Alvaj checked his timepiece. "We should head farther in. More troops will be arriving soon. While they handle the city, we should make certain that the Yajixa doesn't escape."

Avala nodded.

"We'll come with you!" Echniath said in excitement. "You won't be able to defeat the Yajixa without us!"

Alvaj sighed in resignation. "Fine. But be careful, we don't want to lose either of you." They both giggled. "What?" he asked, glaring at them.

"You forget that if these bodies die, we'll just make replacements," Elizba said. "And it took far too much effort for the Yajixa to steal us from our bodies in the first place. There's no way they'll be able to replicate it any time soon."

Alvaj smacked his forehead, the same strange human expression that Avala had seen before. "Well, I guess there's no stopping you."

The girls giggled harder, and Avala found it hard not to join in. "Let's go," she said, smiling. "We came here for a reason. Let's make certain we do what we're supposed to."

10

FREEDOM

"Ah, I have fond memories of these halls," Echniath said, sighing as they walked down a nondescript tunnel. "This entire structure was the great library where we wrote our prophecies for our followers. Countless prophecies were stored here. Alas, those who came after us turned it into a place for the dead."

"The decorations we chose did not help with that," Elizba added. "Skulls and bones. What could mere mortals possibly think that means other than death?"

"What was it supposed to mean?" Avala asked. She wondered if it had to do with how Echniath first appeared when she met her in her mind.

"Bones are the frame that all bodies are built upon," Echniath replied. "We figured it was apt symbolism. It represents the bones of our civilization—the frame that all else was built on."

Alvaj nodded as he looked around. "I guess I can see that."

Moments later, the tunnel shook violently, as if rocked by a massive explosion.

"What was that?" Avala cried.

"It felt like a bomb went off deeper in the ruins," Alvaj replied. "There weren't supposed to be any bombs!"

"We'll find out what it was; no need to panic now," Avala said, trying to calm him.

"Come on, we have to move faster," Alvaj urged.

They jogged down the winding tunnel until they reached what should have been the place where Daigix was entombed, only nothing was there but a massive void.

"What in the world happened here?" Alvaj asked.

Avala's face echoed his remark. Nothing was there—literally. The void appeared to be perfectly spherical, which was odd.

"Stay back." Alvaj picked up a loose rock and threw it into the void. It disintegrated with a loud pop. "It's as I feared," he said. "This is an obliteration field. Nothing can enter it without meeting the same fate as that rock."

"The Yajixa must have escaped and rigged the place to explode," Echniath said. "Something else probably triggered it by mistake, and that saved us!"

"So much for getting to him before he escaped," Avala said.

"What? Are you kidding? Have you forgotten about us?" Elizba asked, insulted.

"What could you possibly do?" Alvaj inquired.

Echniath crossed her arms smugly. "Turn back time."

Avala and Alvaj looked at her in disbelief. She couldn't be serious, could she?

Echniath and Elizba turned to each other and placed their hands together, palm to palm. Their eyes began to glow a bright blue. When they spoke, it was in one voice coming from two mouths, the same voice as when Avala met Echniath in her mind. "We see the two mortals and our drones. We see them in a bubble. We see time stay still in the bubble. We see time turn backward around the bubble. We see the ruins be un-consumed by oblivion. We see the detonation device being un-triggered. We see the Yajixa un-leave the chamber. We see the detonation device being un-placed. We see the

Yajixa being un-informed. We see time go forwards again. We see the bubble release the mortals and drones."

In an instant, everything around them changed. They were in the same location, but the void in the ruins was gone, replaced with what should have been there. Inside the room was a nobleman and his servants. Someone noticed the four of them appear and screamed, pointing at them. "Them! The murderers of Daigix! They've come to desecrate his grave!"

The nobleman turned and looked at them, rage in his eyes. He looked at Avala, boring right into her mind. "Murderer!" he roared. "I see now why we haven't heard from Yvan! You did more than just kill his body! You killed his spirit! He was like a father to me! I'll kill you!"

He charged, pulled out a dagger, and swung it like a madman. Behind her, Avala heard the girls speaking in their ancient voice. A moment later, the nobleman collided with an invisible wall, knocking himself unconscious.

"What they say about her is true! She's a witch who uses the power of the Devalra!" one of the servants yelled in fear.

The two girls behind Avala continued to chant, and the servants continued to panic. But soon the world around Avala slipped away, and she found herself falling as her legs collapsed.

When she opened her eyes, she was still falling. Below her were the structures of her mindscape, and she was approaching them far too fast. Before she could stop herself, she crashed through the roof, right into the chamber where she first met Echniath. Inside was a scared young Yajiran. He screamed as she landed next to him.

"Please, don't kill me!" he cried. "I don't want to die!"

Avala wanted to kill him, but she stopped herself. He was not fighting her like Yvan was. This one was but a child compared to him. He must have known that she was his killer and that he was helpless compared to Yvan. She looked at him, willing her eyes to spot the source of his power, the Echarikith inside him. She spotted a ball of light, where his heart should have been.

She was about to reach for it when she realized that was what killed Yvan. She reached out her hand and willed a living, beating heart into it. Then she carefully replaced the glowing ball of light with the beating heart. The Yajiran did not die but continued to shake in terror. He was alive, like she had hoped. Holding the ball of light in her hand, she willed a portal into the void to open in the floor beneath the Yajiran. She threw the ball of light into the opening after him.

She expected to awake once she was finished, but instead, a voice called out from the void. "Thank you for freeing me. Allow me to join my mind to yours. If I do not, they will surely destroy me for leaving them. I beg you, protect me!" It was the voice of the Yajiran whom she had just freed.

She nodded and established a link to the Yajiran's mind. She willed the door to be outside the prison room, in a location she deemed defensible. Then she willed herself to the door and opened it. Inside was a masterpiece of architecture, though relatively small compared to Yvan's. Inside, the Yajiran was already freeing all who had been enslaved. He smiled and waved for her to come in. She entered and found herself in the Yajiran's mind.

"Welcome. I'm so glad you allowed me to link to you. It gave me the power to close the links to the other Yajixa. I'm freeing everyone I can here. My parents, rest their souls, would never have approved of this." He looked at her hopefully. "Unfortunately, the tortured beast that was here must have escaped my mind. After everything they made me put it through, I don't think it's going to be safe to walk free."

"That 'beast' was one of the Echarikith. I freed it, as was my intention all along," Avala replied.

"Wait! That was one of the Ancients?" his face went pale. "My parents would kill me! We Athakri revere them!"

"You're an Athakri?" Avala asked. "How did the Yajixa get their hands on you?"

"When our world fell to them, I was only twelve by our planet's years, when my parents were killed. The humans of the colony said I was more like eleven and five-sixths by their calendar, but the number didn't matter to me. I was still too young."

Avala was quiet. She just looked at him, feeling his sadness.

"When I was older, they took me from the others. They did something to me, and I found myself in this place. When I awoke, I felt the work of their enslavement on me. I found myself doing things that I felt were wrong, but I could not oppose them. Whenever I entered my mind, I found that beast chained in the heart of the place. At first I thought it was what enslaved me. But then I noticed the things attached to it, tendrils that lead to other mindscapes. I felt the connections break when you freed me.

"Now there's a giant beating heart there instead," he said, looking at her accusingly, "though I admit it still pumps life to the rest of my mind. The tendrils are also gone, and I was able to shut out the mindscapes they connected to. But still, you had to replace it with a heart?"

"It was in the right place." Avala shrugged, knowing she would not be able to explain.

He shook his head and sighed. "I guess I should introduce myself. I'm Evyn."

"I'm Avala. Pleased to meet you," she replied.

Evyn looked around at his mindscape. "I think I've done what I can in here. Why don't we leave?"

Suddenly, Avala felt herself being pulled backward, as if by a vacuum. Her eyes flew open. She was back in the City of Bones, exactly where she had passed out. In fact, her body was still falling to the ground. She landed hard against the stone.

She picked herself up and looked around. The nobleman was coming to as well. He sat up and looked at her, smiling. "Free at last!" he said. Several servants rushed over and pulled him to safety. "No, my people. This woman is no witch! She saved me from brutal enslavement by the spirits. She did it not with the power of the Devalra but because she is one of the Yaji." Several of the servants gasped and murmured among themselves. He stood up, rubbing a bump on his head. "Avala, I hope you will allow me to apologize to you. It seems I have my life, thanks to you. May the ancients smile upon you."

As he spoke, Avala saw Echniath and Elizba glaring at her. "You were supposed to kill him!" Echniath yelled.

"What happened to our kin?" Elizba demanded.

"Up here!" a singsong voice said from above. Avala looked up to see a male humanoid creature with massive bat-like wings protruding from his back sitting on a ledge. Unlike the other two Echarikith, he was not in the body of a child.

"Not him!" Echniath yelled. "Can you put him back where you found him, please?"

"What's wrong with Noochi?" Elizba asked. "I think he's kind of cool."

"He's crazy! He always takes the strangest bodies and makes a fool of himself. He once made a drone that was a tiny insect and kept stinging me! It was all I could do not to swat him," Echniath said.

Noochi swung down, so his talons held him upside down from the ledge, bringing him to eye level with Echniath. "Yeah, but you're the one who always makes child drones since you changed genders. How is that not crazy?" He laughed.

"Noochi! You have to behave yourself! We have to free our kin, and we don't need you messing things up!" Echniath yelled in her childish way.

"The way we treat each other, it's no wonder nobody believes we share the same consciousness," Elizba said quietly.

"'Same' is a bit strong of a word, sister. I think the phrase you're looking for is 'intrinsically connected,'" Noochi said, smirking.

"Will you all just behave? We have a city to take!" Alvaj roared in frustration.

Avala agreed with him. They still had a lot of work ahead of them before the city was theirs. She just hoped the two girls wouldn't kill the newcomer before they took it.

11
WHERE AM I?

As they approached the main city area, they heard the sounds of battle and people screaming in panic about the Devalra attacking and begging the spirits to protect them from death. Little did anyone realize the soldiers were not killing anyone, just knocking them unconscious. When they awoke next, the city would be under the Republic's control.

"I can't believe he just ran off like that," Elizba said.

"I can," Echniath replied. "He doesn't seem to understand the need to free our kin! I'm glad he left. At least he won't cause us any trouble."

"Quiet, you two. The city is up ahead," Alvaj said. He placed a hand to his ear, where a small device was located. "We need to be careful. If I'm hearing this right, Bone Lord Dargoth may, in fact, be a Yajixa."

"How do they know?" Avala asked. She still was not used to all this advanced technology, so she wondered if they had a device that could tell them. Either that or they had brought some of the Athakri with them. They always seemed to be able to tell a Yajixa when they saw one.

"He seems to know too much. Essentially, he used the word 'human.' Your people don't know what that word means, but the Yajixa do," Alvaj said quietly.

"He might have heard it from somewhere else," Echniath suggested.

Avala agreed. It was not enough information to say for certain whether he was a Yajixa, but Alvaj was right; they had to be careful.

The tunnel opened into a massive cavern lined with many levels of walkways and buildings along the edges. They appeared to be on one of the upper levels. Several massive bridges spanned the width of the cavern, connected in the center by a large tower hanging from the ceiling. Even from where she stood, Avala saw countless bodies lying on the ground. The screaming was dwindling, probably because few were still conscious.

Soldiers advanced across the bridges toward the tower. Bone Lord Dargoth was most likely inside. Avala half expected the bridges to collapse as the soldiers crossed them, but they remained firm. Obviously, the people in the tower hadn't thought about destroying the bridges. There must not have been any other way in or out; otherwise, it would have been a great move. In fact, the soldiers were all using harnesses and cables connecting them to solid ground in case the bridges were rigged with traps.

"We should head for the tower," Alvaj stated.

Before they could, a sound like thunder echoed through the cavern. They watched as the tower was disconnected at the top by explosives. The bridges could not hold the weight of the tower and started collapsing.

Avala heard the two girls behind her start speaking in their ancient voice, and she expected the tower to freeze in place, or something to that effect, but all that happened was the soldiers were thrown back to safety. Avala looked down at her feet and sighed as the tower crashed into the cavern floor, breaking to pieces.

"Sorry, we couldn't do anything else," Echniath said, sensing their disappointment. "Our power has its limits. Maybe if there were more of us, we could have stopped the tower."

"Why couldn't you just reverse time, like you did back there?" Alvaj asked, obviously frustrated.

Elizba sighed. "The two of us alone would not have been able to push time back far enough. We know the explosives were already primed when the soldiers arrived. They were rigged to fire when a door to the tower opened. There was nothing we could have done."

Avala understood now. The Bone Lord must have been warned of their arrival and activated a defense mechanism. She knew only the Yajixa were brave enough to rig something like that. Everyone inside most likely died. That wouldn't have been a loss for a Yajixa. They would have absorbed the souls and fled to a new body. That meant if the Bone Lord was a Yajixa, he had already fled to another body, probably one in the city.

"He could be in any of these people," Avala said.

Alvaj nodded. "This is going to be a nightmare, attempting to find which one."

"Incoming!" Avala looked up at the source of the voice to see Noochi flying toward them with a bundle in his talons. Upon closer inspection, she realized the bundle was a man clothed in furs and bones. Noochi dropped the man at their feet before colliding with Echniath, knocking her backward. "Sorry for that. Couldn't stop, you see." He snickered.

"I hate you. You know that?" Echniath growled, picking herself up.

"I found this oaf in the tower. I recognized him as one of the Yajixa," Noochi said, resting a foot on the man. "I can't seem to free our kin from within him, but I know this lovely young lady was able to free me." He looked at Avala in a way that made her feel sick.

"Is he still alive?" Alvaj asked, checking the man's pulse. "Yep, seems like he is."

"Well, what are we waiting for?" Avala asked.

The three Echarikith looked at each other for several moments. Finally, Echniath spoke. "We are finding transferring these Yajixa to your mind quite risky. You see, your mind might not be able to handle it for much longer."

"Why not?" Avala asked. She did not feel like anything was wrong with her mind.

"Your mind was damaged when you freed me," Noochi replied. "From what we can tell, your mind is not strong enough to contain the dangers that some of these Yajixa might unleash upon you."

"Even when your prey did not fight, your entrance into your mindscape damaged something," Elizba continued. "If the barriers to your mind are that weak, it's going to be difficult to contain another strong spirit."

"What do you suggest I do then?" Avala asked.

The three of them looked at each other again, as if silent words were being passed between them. "We need to strengthen your mind," Echniath said. "Build up defenses. We're the ones who are going to enter your mind. Our power together should be enough, at least for now."

"We need your permission first though," Elizba said.

Avala thought about it. What could go wrong? She couldn't think of anything. But for some reason, the thought of those beings entering her mind scared her. Something was wrong about it. They were hiding something from her. There was a danger associated with them entering her mind. There had to be.

"What aren't you telling me?" she asked.

Again the three of them looked at each other. Noochi was the first to speak. "If we leave our bodies, they will gain minds of their own. We cannot claim them again."

"They would be lost and confused, with no knowledge of who or what they are," Elizba added.

"And they may not all be friendly," Echniath said.

Avala nodded. She would not ask it of them. She sighed. "I'll do it myself. Don't lose those bodies for my sake. Besides, this is no place for young children."

They nodded in unison. "Then allow us to help you enter your mind," Echniath said.

Avala took a deep breath. "Okay then."

The three of them started chanting in their ancient voice. Avala felt herself drift off to sleep, as if she was floating downwards on a cloud.

She felt her body land softly on the ground. She opened her eyes to an unrecognizable area. It was not her mind as she recognized it. In fact, she wasn't certain it was a mindscape at all. The sky seemed bright, and a strange glowing circle was in the middle of it. She was resting on a stone floor in a city. All around her, as far as she could see, statues of creatures big and small stood in awe.

She stood up and called for help. She couldn't even hear her own voice. She recognized two of the statues. They were of Echniath and Elizba, standing side by side looking past her. She noticed all the statues were looking the same way, and all seemed to have a look of horror on their face. She looked in that direction and saw, in the distance, a city-sized rock, frozen in time as it crashed into the world.

She stared in horror at the rock as it started moving, as if time began to move again. She prepared for the worst until she realized the rock was going back up into the sky, the damage being undone. The statues started moving as well as they all started looking away.

Moments later she found herself in a busy town filled with people and creatures. Suddenly, two young girls collided with her, and Avala stumbled, quickly catching herself. They were Echniath and Elizba. They looked up at her, and their eyes went wide in fear.

"What are you doing on our world, lesser one?" Echniath demanded. Everyone around her stopped and looked at Avala, their eyes glowing. Pain roared through her head. Avala fell to her knees; it felt as if her head was exploding. The world went black as cold embraced her.

12

THE DISTANT PAST

Avala awoke to the sound of hushed voices. Something dark was covering her eyes. When she tried to sit up, she realized bonds were holding her.

"Trying to escape is pointless," Echniath said from beside her.

"Why are you doing this?" Avala cried. Echniath was her friend; she could not fathom why she would turn on her.

"Why did you come to our world? How did you get here?" Elizba asked from Avala's other side.

"What do you mean by 'your world'?" Avala felt tears in her eyes. "Last I remembered, we were in the City of Bones, which is on my world!"

"What are you talking about? What City of Bones?" Echniath asked.

"Don't you remember? You were there! The three of you were trying to send me to my mind. I was going to make it stronger, so I could better fight the Yajixa!" Avala was so confused. Were they messing with her?

"She appears to be a cast-off, but I can't think of who created her," Echniath said to Elizba.

"Maybe she was only recently awakened as a lesser being," Elizba suggested.

"No. Her memories are plenty. I see . . . ." Avala felt something strange in her mind as Echniath gasped. "She's not from our time." Her voice changed to her ancient one, and she began to recite the prophecy Avala first saw in the City of Bones. "We see the girl, Avala. We see she will awaken us after we fall. We see she is a half-breed. We see that she takes part in a war. We see that she becomes a shifter of bodies. We see that she becomes a collector of souls. We see the girl, Avala. We see that she will awaken us after we fall."

Elizba gasped. "Echniath! You just . . . you just spoke in the voice of the Consciousness!"

Echniath laughed. "I did, didn't I? Maybe it'll make it into the Great Library of Ecrekio, though I doubt it. I don't know what came over me. I was just looking into her mind. Then I saw something that indicated she was from the future. And then the voice came over me. It was wonderful."

"I'm from the future?" Avala asked sadly. "How far?"

"Three long cycles, it seems," Echniath replied.

"What's a long cycle?" As Avala asked it, she felt something sifting through her thoughts.

"You come from the world that Ecrekio is on?" Elizba asked.

"Yes. That's where the City of Bones is."

"Then each long cycle is a million of your years," Elizba replied.

Avala started to cry. She was so far from home. So far in the past. Her people didn't even exist yet. The humans of the Republic were probably still primitives, or maybe not even that. Everyone she knew, other than the Echarikith, weren't born yet. "How did I get here?" she asked through her tears.

"We don't know," Echniath replied, taking the blindfold off Avala's face and undoing the bonds that held her in place. "You said we were going to send you to your mind? How were we going to accomplish that?"

"You were going to speak using that strange voice to cause it to happen. I don't know how it works though. Please, I just want to go home." Avala continued to cry.

"We were using the voice of the Consciousness?" Echniath asked Elizba. "But only the rarest of Echarikith can use it at will!"

"Well, I don't know what the 'different voice' is that she would be talking about other than that," Elizba replied.

"Whatever it is—" Echniath was cut off when the two of them clutched their heads and started shouting in their ancient voice simultaneously. In fact, outside the room they were in, Avala heard countless people shouting the same words with the same voice. The voice was filled with terror.

"We see the end! We see the bringer of death! We see the rock from above! We see it fall on our world! We are afraid! Our core is threatened! Our life is threatened! We must flee! We must escape!"

As they shouted, the two girls walked out of the room, as if in a trance, and onto the street. Avala followed. They and countless others looked up at the sky. As they finished speaking, Avala saw what they were looking at: a city-sized rock coming from the clouds. Moments later everything went cold as wisps of energy emerged from every single creature in sight. They darted into the sky, hundreds of colored lights shooting upwards.

Then the rock hit. The ground exploded around it and sent a shockwave through the entire world. Avala watched as a young teenage girl in front of her was blasted backward and directly through her. She turned to see what happened to her. Only then did she realize it was her own body she had seen. She was dead.

The world around her collapsed in on itself, dying before her eyes. She felt her mind implode on itself. And then all was dark.

But it was not the end. Her spirit wandered through the stars. She drifted endlessly, searching for a body. Many were found, but she rejected them all. Each one had a life of its own. Each one was someone else. She wanted to be herself, to be home.

Ages passed, and she began to forget who she was and where she was from. After countless centuries of wandering, something tugged at the edges of her spirit. Another mind. A voice of ancient power. It drew her forward through time and space.

She found herself looking at a cavern city. Five beings stood around an unconscious figure. Two of the figures were little girls. One was a man. One was a strange creature. And the last was a young teenage girl. The scene seemed vaguely familiar, as if she had been there before.

She saw the teen girl's body go limp and her spirit leave it. She felt drawn toward the body, as if it were her own. She hesitated. Was she ready for her search to end? Was it the right body? She could not resist the pull of the voice urging her forward.

As she entered the body, it felt familiar. Suddenly, it clicked. This was *her* body, her original body. How long had she been away from it? Her spirit settled in, and feeling returned to her limbs.

Avala's eyes flew open, and she screamed. The last thing she remembered was the massive rock slamming into the ground. She looked around expecting to see the ruins of a world. Instead, she found herself back in the City of Bones. Echniath and Elizba came to her side. She looked at the two girls, who were smiling.

"You! You sent me . . . to the past!" she cried. She had witnessed the death of a world. Had it been a nightmare? It felt so real.

"We're sorry we tricked you, but we needed to send you there. Otherwise my prophecy would never have been made," Echniath said quietly.

"I could have died!" Avala said, no longer sad but angry.

"You did. Your spirit wandered for millennia before we brought you back," Elizba replied softly.

Avala tried to remember. Slowly she began to recall the travels of her spirit in the time before she returned to her body. She had questions about what she experienced on that dying world. "What were all those lights right before the end?"

"Those were our spirits leaving the bodies of our drones. We were fleeing the destruction of our world. The meteor destroyed it, wiping away all life from the surface. We created new bodies elsewhere," Echniath said. "Unfortunately, even those not on our home world accidentally fled their bodies, creating many of the sapient species of the galaxy."

"Back then, you acted as if using that different voice of yours on purpose was nearly impossible," Avala said. "Why is it different now?"

Elizba sighed. "This is going to sound weird, but the Echarikith are actually one massive mind. It is split into countless parts, each with its own consciousness, which gives us personality and individuality. But in truth, when we really need to, the Consciousness uses our bodies for its greater purpose. Since right now only three of us are free to do anything, we are being used far more frequently."

It took a few moments for Avala to process what she meant, but once she did, she thought she understood.

Alvaj, who had been silent until then, sighed. "I'm not going to pretend to understand what you're talking about, but I'm curious if we can do what we need to with this crazy old man before he wakes up."

Elizba and Echniath looked at each other and nodded. "Your mind should have strengthened over the millennia," Echniath said to Avala. "We can proceed."

"No more tricks, please?" Avala asked.

Elizba smiled. "We promise. No more tricks."

The two girls and Noochi began chanting in their ancient voice again. As they did, Avala, who hadn't even sat up yet, fell asleep. She felt like she was gently floating down a river on a boat.

Avala opened her eyes and sat up. She seemed to indeed be on a small boat that had floated through the void in her mind, directly to a doorway. With a thought, she was on the other side of the door. Inside was a magnificent, chaotic city, sprawling in almost every direction. It was nothing like she remembered. Ages must have passed to produce such detail. A figure approached her. She recognized it as Vran.

"Avala! You grace us with your presence after so incredibly long! We have done much in your time away." He embraced her.

"If my mindscape has changed so much, what about Evyn's, whose mind is connected to mine?" Avala asked.

As if to answer her question, Evyn came walking toward her. "It seems whenever you enter your mindscape, so do I—at least some part of me. It seems my mind has changed significantly since I was last in it. People here in your mindscape tell me that you went time traveling! Is that true?"

Avala nodded. "The Echarikith sent me to the fall of their world. I died there, but after millennia of wandering without a body, they pulled me back to my own body in the present."

"You went millennia without a body? Wow, I've only ever gone a few moments," he said. "Though I guess you're in here for a reason. Is it another Yajixa?"

She nodded. "This one might not be friendly."

"We'll see," Evyn said. "Shall we proceed?"

She nodded and willed herself, Evyn, and Vran to the entrance of the prison. Then she willed it to open. Inside was an old Yajiran man dressed in furs and bones. He looked at her and growled in anger.

"You have made a mistake imprisoning me in your mind, child! I will make you fear!"

As he spoke, a rift opened in the air. Inside, Avala saw countless creepy creatures and skeletal people. The monsters began entering her mind, and she screamed in fear.

13

ENTRALLIA

Avala ran through the city of her mindscape. She was chasing the Yajixa, who had escaped the prison chamber. She had let her guard down for one moment too long. Now he was wreaking havoc throughout her mindscape.

Everywhere the Yajixa went, he opened rifts to his own mindscape, unleashing its horrors upon hers. She knew all she had to do was free the Echarikith inside him to stop him, but she could not get close enough. Every time she stopped to close a rift, he got a little farther ahead.

All around her, inhabitants of the city were putting aside their daily lives to defend their home. She saw far more people in her mind that she expected. Had she somehow absorbed more during her time away, or were they capable of reproducing within her mind? She shook her head. Now was not the time to try to understand it. She had to find a way to stop the Yajixa.

It was as she was closing a rift that the idea hit her. She would lead a force of her strongest through one of the rifts. They would end the Yajixa from in there.

She used her will to summon all the strongest fighters from within her mind. With a thought, she explained her plan, indicating it was voluntary. Nearly 100 of the 130 decided to come with her. The rest she placed back where they came from, so they could continue to defend. As she led the group to a nearby rift, she knew it would be like stepping into a nightmare. And it was.

The world beyond was filled with larvae, insects, corpses, and a number of other strange monstrosities. As the group followed her through, many of them were preparing for the worst. Avala tested out her force of will in that place, wanting to make certain she could do something if things went sour. Fortunately, she still had limited control. It must have been similar to what the Yajixa was capable of.

She looked around, trying to judge what to do next. The place seemed small compared to her own mind when she had first entered it so long ago. In fact, a short distance away, they saw a towering skeletal figure. It was being tortured by countless strands of energy that kept impaling its body. It roared in pain as every tendril touched it. Its appearance reminded her of the way she first saw Echniath, and she realized it was an Echarikith.

"We need to free that thing!" she yelled to the others. "That is our primary objective!"

"Secondary objective is to survive!" Vran called out from beside her. "We may not be unkillable in another person's mind." Then he raised his sword. "For Avala! For victory! For freedom!"

The others echoed his cry and charged. Avala watched them from where she was. She seemed to have more control with her willpower near the rift than she did farther away. She wanted every advantage possible, so staying there seemed like the best option.

The warriors pushed through. Every time a warrior got severely wounded, she used her will to open a temporary rift to her mindscape beneath them. Once the power of her mind healed them, she brought them back into the fray.

Vran led the warriors, inspiring them and keeping morale high. He kept them focused on the task, leaping to the defense of warriors as they fell. He seemed unstoppable.

Eventually, the warriors reached the trapped Echarikith. Now the monsters of the mindscape were focused on stopping them. The creatures that had not yet been defeated in her mindscape began pouring through the rifts. Some came through the rift right beside her but ignored her, focusing instead on her fighters.

The warriors slashed at several of the tendrils, severing them and causing the creatures to react more frantically. Avala tried to use her will to help by making a ring of rifts around them, blocking most of the monsters on the ground. As her warriors slashed at the tendrils, the Echarikith looked directly at her. She did not know how she recognized it, but she saw hope in its expression.

Finally, as the last of the tendrils was severed, the Echarikith roared in fury. "We have been released! We will make those who hurt us suffer!" It charged through the monsters, directly at Avala. She felt someone place a hand on her shoulder and a blade point on her back.

"Go back to your cage, slave, or your hero dies!" the Yajixa behind her yelled.

The Echarikith halted, fear in its eyes—fear of losing the only hope for its kind. Avala closed her eyes, preparing for the end. She waited, but it never came. Instead a scream came from behind her as the hand and blade were ripped away from her. She turned to see Vran tackling the Yajixa in a stranglehold, his own blade across its chest.

"Nobody threatens my sister!" he yelled, slitting the Yajixa's chest.

The mindscape around them imploded, and Avala felt herself being crushed. Moments later the feeling passed, and she found herself back in her own mindscape. The other warriors were there as well, looking around, confused. The rift, through which she had first entered stood sputtering and crackling to the side. It must have ejected them during the Yajixa's death throes. She used her will to stabilize the rift, but she put a heavy gate on it to protect those in her own mindscape from its dangers.

She sensed the nightmare mindscape beyond was now part of her mind. It would be used as a place for her warriors to train. Feeling other rifts elsewhere in her mind, she stabilized and gated each of them as well.

Behind her, she sensed the Echarikith, most likely waiting for release. Without turning to it, she opened a gate to the void for it. It stayed put. Turning to it, she questioned it with a thought as to why it stayed.

"We will stay and release the portion of Echniath she left behind," it said. "We will stay to help you free others. We will stay to protect you. We will make our new body in your mind."

Avala watched as the Echarikith became a ball of light that turned into the form of a person. When the light faded, Avala saw a beautiful teenage Athakarin girl about her own age. The girl looked almost identical to her, the only differences being her hair and her eyes were red.

"I am Entrallia," the girl said, bowing. "I was once the caretaker of the Great Library of Ecrekio. I am now the keeper of your power." She smiled at Avala.

Avala smiled back and then closed the gateway to the void. "Welcome to my mind, Ancient One. May you feel at home here."

"Your friends are expecting you. You should return to them," Entrallia replied.

Avala nodded, finding herself falling backward.

Her eyes flew open. She looked around, and found that she was lying on hearth pillows in a home carved out of stone. She sat up, spotting Echniath glaring at her.

"She stayed! Didn't she?" the girl asked.

It took Avala a moment to understand what she meant. Once she did, she nodded, "That Yajixa was tough. When we defeated it, I tried to let her go, but she said she wanted to stay. I couldn't make her leave."

"Figures." Echniath sighed. "Well, at least my entire spirit is out here now. I should feel happy for her sacrifice, but I'm not. She was the one who gave me a home after our core was destroyed. She let me stay here in Ecrekio, since I had made a prophecy. She trained me in harnessing the Consciousness, so I could prophesy more. I'll miss her."

Avala looked at the ground, trying to think of what to say. Finally, she looked up. "What happened to the Lord of Bones?"

"He crumbled to dust. It appears he was little more than a withered corpse, kept alive only by the spirit inside him. He could not live on his own. Sad, but it fits with the Yajixa. I saw his mind through the Consciousness. It was terrifying." Echniath shuddered. "It appears he only claimed the souls of the long dead. He must have been the one who ensured that no soul was left unclaimed. He also had an obsession with all things creepy. I'm glad he's gone."

Avala looked around for the others but saw no sign of them. "Where is everyone?"

"Working to help teach the rest of the city the truth about the 'spirits.' It's going to take some time." She sighed. "In the weeks you've been asleep, a resistance group has taken up residence among the tower's remains. They are led by the city's priests and priestesses and have been causing all sorts of problems."

"Are there any Yajixa among them?"

"No. We seem to have taken care of all the Yajixa here." Echniath still seemed worried. "Though one could easily awaken in any of the people here. All they would have to do is release themselves from their current body and make their way here. The humans are lucky; only those descended from the cast-offs of the Echarikith can be taken over by a Yajixa. The humans originated independently from us, unlike many races of the galaxy."

"What created the humans?" Avala asked.

"It happened a long time after our fall. The Yajirans did not find them in time to take total control. I don't know how they came about, but I know they are lucky in so many ways.

"Nearly five thousand of their years ago, the Yajixa infiltrated their governments, using bodies similar to humans. Because of the well-established human religions, the Yajixa could not manipulate them in their normal way. Instead, the Yajixa caused countless wars, killing billions and then absorbing their souls.

"Nearly a thousand years later, they were still causing trouble when humans launched the first probes into the stars. Half a century after that, one of their greatest nations had its leader replaced with one of the Yajixa. He, along with most of the world leaders, who were also replaced by Yajixa, tried to start another major world war. He was caught in the act of discussing plans to destroy humanity with the other leaders, revealing they were aliens, thanks to the intervention of an expert hacker. It was then that the humans became aware of the Yajixa.

"The Yajixa were rooted out, and their technology was stolen, including MELT technology, which eliminated the need for space travel to reach different worlds. The humans made it their mission to protect primitive worlds from the Yajixa. Though it wasn't until two thousand years ago that they found the Yajirans, the original race of the Yajixa, and that was only after finding the Athakri. The Echarikith consciousness witnesses everything the Yajixa do, so we know most of what happened."

Avala nodded. As she looked out the doorway, she saw three wisps of red energy fly through the cavern. Her eyes widened as she realized what they were. The Yajixa had sent backup, and any of the Athakarins there could be it.

14

THE AVALANS

Avala and Echniath rushed into the cavern city in hopes of finding the Yajixa before it was too late. A scream came from a nearby home, and orange blood pouring out from the doorway. Avala rushed to the home and looked inside, expecting to find a Yajixa. Instead she found the corpse of a woman, holding a bloody knife in her hand. The expression on the woman's face was that of confusion and terror.

"It looks like she killed herself," Echniath said solemnly. "The Yajixa must be possessing people and killing them."

"Why would they do that?" Avala asked, feeling a lump in her throat.

"To lessen our victory," Echniath replied. "We spared these people to teach them the truth about their world. Killing them makes our attempts futile."

Avala felt tears in her eyes again. The Yajixa didn't care about anyone but themselves. They were willing to kill innocents just to stop the plans of Avala and her friends. She heard more screams. Each cry filled her with hopelessness. She could not stop this. She was powerless on her own, and given the recent struggle in her mind, she knew she could not take on as many Yajixa as were now attacking the city.

"Avala," Echniath said, "we have to do something?"

Avala could only cry. She did not have the power to save her people. She was wrong to think she could. The Yajixa were willing to use tactics that she could not fight. They were ruthless. How could she stop them? She looked at Echniath, "It's hopeless. I can't save them. Not by myself."

"We have to try." Echniath's eyes began to glow, and her voice changed as she began to chant. A terrible crashing sound echoed through the cavern, and the ground began to shake. Wisps of energy poured through the cavern entrances.

A great light exploded around them, forcing her eyes closed. When the light faded, Avala opened her eyes again. She was still in the city, but something was different. Rubble and other loose objects floated through the air. At first she thought she was in her mind, but then she saw Echniath beside her.

The screaming had stopped. In fact, everything seemed silent. She tested her voice, and she could still hear it. She clapped her hands, and it still made a sound. She realized the natural ambiance of the cavern was missing.

She looked around. Over a dozen Yajirans lay unconscious on the ground. They had not been there before. Where had they come from? She turned to Echniath. "What happened? How did those Yajirans get here?"

"We're in your mind," she replied.

"What do you mean?" Avala asked.

"We brought the cavern into your mind, and in doing so stopped the Yajixa," Echniath explained.

Avala gasped. If those Yajiran were Yajixa, then she had to stop them before they awoke. With a thought, she was at the nearest one. It looked like a young girl. Avala reached for her heart. Before she could grab it, the girl woke up, screaming in terror. Picking herself up, she ran away.

The other Yajirans also started waking up. Avala noticed that many of them seemed awfully young. They all looked terrified and quickly huddled together for safety.

As Avala approached them, the oldest stepped in front of the group defensively. "I will not let you hurt them," the young man growled.

"I don't seek to hurt anyone," Avala said. "It was you who were killing people."

"They were being bad!" one of the nearest young ones said.

"We are the rightful rulers of the galaxy!" the eldest declared. "We can kill whoever we want! But I will not let you continue to hurt my people!"

Avala sighed. She had hoped these Yajixa would be like Evyn. Instead, they seemed loyal to their people and cause. She could not kill them though, since some of them were children. They must have been newly initiated Yajixa, sent en masse to stop them.

She could not kill them, but she also could not leave the Echarikith inside them. She closed her eyes. She could not make this impossible choice. Replacing their hearts with a true heart might have saved Yvan, but these Yajixa weren't in an body. They would surely perish.

She had to try something. She willed a fist-sized crystal into her hand. With a thought, she made the crystal into an eternal power source. She willed it to replace the heart of the Yajiran in front of her. He did not seem to notice as the ball of light was now in her hands. She placed it on the ground. Then she repeated the same process for each of the other Yajiran. The crystals would allow them to keep the power of the Yajixa but not be slaves to their ideals. Slowly, they realized something was different.

The lead one blinked. "I don't hear their voice anymore. You . . . freed us?"

Avala nodded.

"We were all just children when we were taken from our parents," he said. "Each one of us had shown signs of being a Yajixa. It was exciting at first, thinking we would be able to be like the heroes of legends. None of us realized we had been lied to about what the Yajixa really did. When we became like them . . . the horrors that we inflicted on others . . . we realized we were the bad guys. The Yajixa aren't heroes! They're monsters! And we were forced to be like them."

The others murmured in agreement.

Avala heard chanting from the Echarikith as the world around them started to shake again. Within moments they were all knocked to the ground. When Avala opened her eyes, the ambient noise of the cavern was back. Reality had been restored. The Yajirans were also gone. Most likely it had been their spirits in the mindscape, thus they needed new bodies in reality.

Beside her, nearly a dozen beings of different shapes and sizes stood together in a cluster. Echniath, Elizba, and Noochi rushed up to the group, as if they knew them. They began talking and hugging each other like they were at a big family reunion. It likely was, in a sense. She could tell they were all Echarikith.

People emerged from the ruined tower down below, yelling that they surrendered. Further investigation yielded that the group of one-time Yajixa that she had freed moments before had possessed the bodies of the priests and priestesses who had been leading the resistance. Although free from the control of the Ten, they possessed the same powers they had before, through the power of the crystal Avala had placed inside them.

One of the priests knelt in front of Avala, "We no longer serve the Yajixa. We seek to free our people from their grasp, just as you seek to free yours. We offer you our service, if you will accept it."

Avala looked at each of them. They would prove invaluable. She did not have to be the only one anymore. She nodded. "You're going to need something to call yourselves. The word 'Yajixa' won't do anymore."

"You were the first of us," one of them said. "How about we name ourselves after you? We will be called 'Avalans.'" The others nodded in agreement.

Echniath walked up beside her. "I like the name. But the bottom line is, you can't keep those bodies. They don't belong to you. So, we're going to make you new ones, like your originals."

"How are you going to do that?" one of them asked.

"Watch." Echniath smiled, then motioned for the other Echarikith to come over, and they began chanting. Wisps of energy left each of the priests and priestesses' bodies. New Yajiran bodies started forming around each wisp of energy. When it was completed, the new Avalans had their own Yajiran bodies, fully clothed and everything, leaving the priests and priestesses utterly confused.

"Thank you," the oldest of the Avalans said, bowing his head. The others repeated his sentiment.

The next while involved informing Alvaj and Republic Command of all that had taken place. They explained everything as best as they could, though there still seemed to be a great deal of confusion. The priests and priestesses had turned themselves in after seeing their spirits in mortal form. All around, efforts were being made to fortify the city and establish working facilities such as MELT transporters, Adjutant and replicator terminals, and a communications center.

After so much work, Avala grew tired. As she headed toward bed, Alvaj ran up beside her. "Avala, We have a problem!"

"Can it wait?" she asked. "I'm really sleepy."

He shook his head, "A massive force of Yajirans just MELTed in outside the city. They're preparing to attack. They've brought some sort of large device with them. The Echarikith believe it's the same device that originally stole them from their bodies. The Yajirans seem to be planning to use it against them again."

Avala was suddenly afraid. She had worked so hard to free the Echarikith. If the Yajirans planned to steal them from their bodies again, she had to stop them. "They have to get to safety," she replied, stating the obvious.

"That might not be possible. The Yajirans are blocking MELT transportation with a MELT trap. We can't escape. Not to mention there appears to be at least one powerful Yajixa among them. You'll need at least one of the Echarikith to help you stop them."

He had a point. Even though she had Entrallia in her mind, Avala did not know if she would be able to aid in this fight from in there. She sighed. It seemed she would have to fight some more before she could get some sleep.

15

THE BATTLE FOR ECREKIO

"We have to do something!" one of the newly freed Echarikith said, fear in his eyes.

"And we will," Alvaj replied. He had taken charge of the situation. Due to the large force laying siege to the city and the small force they had to defend it, everyone was on edge. The Echarikith were particularly anxious due to the spirit stealer device that the Yajirans had outside. Alvaj was the only one attempting to keep everyone focused on the objective. "The first thing we need to know is how that device works. Does it have a weakness that we can exploit? How close does it have to be to function? How long do we have until it goes off? Unless we can answer those questions, we don't stand a chance."

"We only know that it was the same thing that stole all of us before!" Echniath cried. "We never had the chance to find out more."

"Maybe we can capture someone who knows more?" Avala suggested.

Alvaj nodded. "Not the easiest thing to do. However, unless someone here has any info, we don't have many other options."

Avala, I have an idea, a voice said in her mind. It was Entrallia.

What? Avala responded.

Have my kin take refuge in your mind. They can't be taken by the device that way.

Avala repeated the suggestion aloud.

"Not an option!" Echniath shook her head. "We can't help you from in there. And we sense powerful Yajixa among that army. They'll end up slaughtering all of you without any way to stop them. We can't let that happen."

"You only have to be in there until the device is disabled," Alvaj reminded them, "which we will be able to do far more easily if you're all safe."

The Echarikith looked at each other, then nodded in unison, though it was obvious they did not like the idea. "We will transfer our bodies in as well," Echniath said finally.

"I thought you said you couldn't do that," Avala reminded her.

"We lied," Echniath said.

"It was just an excuse," Elizba clarified.

"Well, just make certain you do it soon. We don't know how much time we have," Alvaj said.

The Echarikith took hold of each other's hands, forming a ring. Their eyes began glowing, each set a different color, as they chanted in their ancient voice. The words seemed alien to Avala, though she recalled that in the past she could understand them. Were they only doing that for her sake? If so, why hide what they were saying?

A massive shockwave shook the cavern, breaking the Echarikiths' concentration. Stumbling to the ground, they clutched their heads, screaming silently in agony. Avala stared in horror as wisps of energy, their very spirits, were slowly ripped from them. Once free, they darted to the surface.

The bodies of the Echarikith collapsed, either unconscious or dead. Avala did not know. What she did know was that the Echarikith had been stolen from their bodies once again. Rage coursed through her. It felt alien to her, as if its original source was not from her. *Entrallia,* she thought. It must be her.

Suddenly, she found herself running toward one of the cavern's exits. She did not know why, but she could guess. Entrallia had taken control of her and was seeking vengeance. *Please stop!* she thought, trying to contact the Echarikith inside her mind. *You're going to get me killed!* No response came.

As she ran, she struggled to gain control of her body. Entrallia wasn't thinking clearly. She was acting on emotions—emotions that were going to get Avala killed. She struggled but found it pointless. The Echarikith was too strong.

She quickly came upon the great staircase leading toward the entrance. She had no weapon; how could she fight an entire army? However, Entrallia didn't seem to care. She was so angry that she was willing to throw Avala at an entire army unarmed in the vain hope of bringing back her people.

Please stop! Avala yelled throughout her mind. *Please, this won't help!* Terror seized her as she neared the top of the staircase.

They must pay! They must suffer! They must die! The words screamed through her mind with burning pain.

As she burst through the gate, Avala flew through the air. The next thing she knew, she was in a body that was not her own and began stabbing it. With sudden realization, she knew what was happening. The Echarikith inside her was using the same tactic the Yajixa had before. She felt pain roar through her new body with each stab. As golden blood poured out from the deadly wounds, she flew out of that body and into another.

This time she began attacking everyone around her with the beam weapon in her hand. It took several moments for others to respond. By the time they turned on her, she had already taken out well over two dozen. As that body fell, she possessed another.

This time she shouted treasonous words about the Yajixa. She claimed they were monsters, murderers, and slavers of their own people. She said horrible things about their leaders and heroes, causing all nearby to attack. As they turned on her in rage, she left that body.

Soon she found her spirit was under her own control again and decided to continue what Entrallia had started. She went from body to body, causing as much mayhem and damage within the enemy ranks as possible.

During a moment when not in a body, she looked to see where her own body was. She spotted it lying on the ground outside the city gate, unmoving and unconscious. She longed to return to it, but she had a job to finish. She possessed person after person, inflicting chaos on the army. Once she was certain she had done enough, she headed for the massive device in the center of the army.

As she possessed the body of the person controlling it, she felt Entrallia search their brain for information. Upon finding what she was looking for, the Echarikith was once again in control. Avala's current body began pressing buttons on the panel. After a few moments, over a dozen wisps of energy flew out of the device. She had released the Echarikith, but she was not done yet.

Avala found Entrallia forcing her to leave the body. She was confused. Did she not have to destroy the device? Her answer presented itself as she soared toward a Yajiran wielding a rocket launcher. After possessing him, she aimed the rocket at the spirit stealer and fired. The rocket exploded the device, sending debris everywhere.

Under her own control again, Avala headed back to her own body. Before she could reach it though, she was pulled in another direction. Some unseen force was drawing her directly toward a Yajiran general. She saw a glimpse into his mind and tried to scream. This Yajiran was a Yajixa, and they were trying to capture her. She struggled in vain as darkness closed in around her.

Avala hit something hard. She was confused. Where was she? She heard water dripping nearby and felt hard stone beneath her. Opening her eyes, she sat up and looked around. She was in a prison cell. Three of the four walls were made of a dark stone, and the fourth consisted of black bars covered in metal spikes. The cold, damp air sent chills through her body.

The last thing she remembered was heading back to her body, then being diverted toward the Yajiran general. Was she in another Yajixa's mind? She looked around for some indication that could confirm her theory but found none.

She looked outside the bars, careful to avoid the spikes. Outside was a massive egg-shaped space lined with row upon row of prison cells. Even if she got past the bars, she would still be trapped.

In frustration, she looked around and spotted a few loose stones on the floor. Grabbing one, she found it felt unnaturally weightless. She threw it outside the bars, but it stopped in midair, right where she released it. That startled her. She grabbed it again, this time simply trying to drop it. It just floated in midair again. Something clicked in her mind. This was the behavior of a mindscape. She was in the Yajixa's mind.

With that thought, she tried opening a rift into her own mind. The back wall tore open, revealing a pathway to her mindscape. Stepping through, she found herself someplace familiar. She was relieved at first, until she saw that everyone around her was pinned to the ground in heavy chains, which she could not seem to remove with her will. As she tested her willpower on other things, nothing obeyed her. She realized, with sudden horror, that she was a prisoner within her own mind, and there was no escape.

16

TURNING
THE TABLES

Avala wandered through her mindscape, trying to find a way out. Everyone she met was unable to help, due to the chains. They also seemed unable to speak, which meant she couldn't learn anything about what had happened. She felt she had been meandering aimlessly for many bell tolls. The place was massive, leaving her hopelessly lost.

She came across several doors that she did not recognize. They were all locked, so she moved on. As time passed, despair overwhelmed her. Was there no way to be free?

She was so lost in hopelessness that she almost missed an open doorway into an unfamiliar mindscape. She looked through the doorway, wondering where it led. She saw a massive device, similar to the one she had destroyed, only a hundred times bigger. Inside were hundreds of Echarikith in their natural form. With horror, she realized it must be the mindscape of one of the original ten Yajixa.

With this revelation, she felt even more hopeless. What could she do against such a powerful mind? Beginning to cry, she curled into a ball next to a wall. There was nothing she could do. She was trapped inside her own mind by a mind that was like a god in comparison.

She was roused from her tears by an armored figure. "Get up! It's time to go!" it said.

She looked up. The being was clearly Yajiran and appeared to be from the Yajixa's mind. Avala felt more tears well up in her eyes and went back to crying. Was the being really so cruel as to take her away from her tears?

The soldier grabbed her arm. She tried to resist, but it was useless. Dragging her by the arm, the soldier proceeded deeper into her mind, toward her prison chamber. Once they arrived, Avala found a young armored Yajiran woman standing outside the door.

"Ah, there she is at last." The woman sighed. "You made quite a mess back there, you know."

Avala hung her head. She wanted to hide and cry. Tears still stung her eyes. As the soldier released her, she collapsed on the floor, sobbing. The woman reached down, putting her hand on her head. "It's okay, dear. You will be safe now. No longer will you have to worry about anything. Look." The woman opened the door.

To Avala's horror, Entrallia was bound by countless chains in the middle of the room. Long tendrils of energy reached out from rifts repeatedly stabbing the Echarikith, causing her to cry out in pain. Avala suddenly knew what they were trying to do. She was going to become their slave, just like every Yajixa she had met. She lowered her head and continued to sob. What could she do?

She looked up and made eye contact with Entrallia. In that moment, she felt a wave of energy flow through her. "We will never give in," she found herself saying. Her own voice sounded alien to her. It felt alien too. It reminded her of something, but at the moment, she couldn't think of what. "We will break these chains. We will close these rifts."

For some reason, the Yajiran woman seemed afraid, but Avala was unable to stop. "We will reverse these bonds. We will be the ones in control. We will capture our captors."

The Yajiran woman panicked, stabbing Avala with a knife and screaming for her to stop. The pain roared through Avala, but she could not stop. The words had to be free, "We will free ourselves. We will not be slaves!" The world around her exploded with lights and sound. Through it all, she heard the woman scream in terror.

When Avala opened her eyes, she felt weak. She was no longer outside Ecrekio; that much was clear. Everything around her was black metal with green glowing highlights. She was sitting on a throne that was far too high for her liking.

She felt sick. Something about the body she was inhabiting felt wrong. She looked at her new hands. They were perfectly smooth, as if they had never seen a moment's work, the fingers adorned with strange rings of green and black.

A man knelt below her. This body could smell his fear, and some part of it liked it. With horror, Avala realized what must have been happening. She was in the body of one of the ten leaders of the Yajixa. What happened to the Yajixa's spirit she did not know, but what she did know was that she did not like this body.

She attempted to leave it but found she could not, and that worried her. What was preventing her from leaving? She searched her new brain for answers but found it empty. It seemed the Yajixa that had owned it previously had been too paranoid to keep any information in it.

She looked at the man on the floor, wondering how she could get the information she wanted without revealing herself. Just then a door at the end of the room opened. In walked a beautiful, young, teenage girl, who appeared about Avala's age.

"Your majesty, you have returned," the girl bowed mockingly at the foot of the throne, as if she had nothing to fear from her. "We heard the battle didn't go as expected, that you failed to capture the Echarikith. I hope for our sake that you have some good news. Do you?"

Avala tensed up. "I have captured the girl, Avala, who has caused us much trouble," she replied.

The girl smiled. "Oh, I can tell. I can also tell that she managed to enslave you and that I am actually speaking to her right now." The girl's grin filled with malice. "Don't try to fool yourself, child. We knew what you did before you even awoke. What did you hope to accomplish? Did you think you could infiltrate the Yajixa as one of their leaders? You're a fool!"

Avala felt fear. The body did not respond well to it. She had hoped to avoid detection, but obviously, she had failed. Unless . . ..

"You dare challenge me?" she yelled. The girl looked taken aback. "You couldn't see into my mind even if you tried! How dare you say that a mere child could possibly enslave me!"

The girl knelt, trembling in fear. "I'm sorry, Mother. It was just a test. You know, in the off chance that she did take control of you. You know I would never dare look into your mind."

Avala had successfully called her bluff. She realized that no person in the Yajiran empire would, as the girl said, look into one of their leader's minds. The girl's insolence must have been from years of being spoiled, thus rarely fearing her mother's wrath.

Though Avala had navigated that well enough, she felt afraid that the next time she wouldn't be so lucky. She sighed. "Avala has proven difficult, I admit. However, after capturing her, it appears I defaulted back to this body. I was not finished my work at Ecrekio and wish to return to finish the job."

"Of course, Mother. Jindyo must have triggered the mind trap field by accident." The girl began beating the man on the floor. "You stupid slave! Can't do anything right, can you?"

Avala had to resist commanding the girl to stop; this had to look natural. The man fell to the floor, a bloody mess. The girl shoved his body aside. "I don't know what you saw in him. He made a horrible father, you know. I'm glad you didn't try to stop me this time. He must have angered you significantly though. I saw you were contemplating stopping me."

She pressed a few buttons on a control panel, "You should be able to leave again. Please come back safe, Mother." The girl smiled maliciously, as if she hoped she didn't return at all.

Avala left that horrible body immediately. While leaving, she saw the girl's eyes go wide with horror. Avala's soul must not have looked anything like what it should have, for the girl attempted to press a few buttons on the control panel in a panicked frenzy. However, Avala was already leaving, flying as far away as she could. She willed herself toward her original body, and the world around her swirled into a maelstrom of light and color. Moments later, she collided with something hard.

Her eyes flew open. She was once again in Ecrekio. Countless people, many she did not know, were standing over her looking solemn. She gasped for air, her lungs burning. The sound and motion caused several people to scream in shock. As people panicked, Elizba and Echniath rushed up and grabbed her hand.

"She's back!" they shouted.

People around them started talking all at once. The mood went from gloom and mourning to rejoicing. She sat up to see all her friends as well as many new faces looking at her in excitement and amazement. They asked her question after question, and she answered what she could. It turned out that they were holding a funeral for her, since they thought she was dead.

Alvaj had found her body after the Echarikith returned to his. He had noticed the Yajiran army in disarray and guessed that she had left her body to stop them. When she returned after quite a while, it was assumed that the Yajixa had killed her spirit.

She explained that one of the Yajixa leaders had captured her. Then she told them all that had happened. Some were suspicious that she was, in fact, under the control of the Yajixa. However, their fears were quickly relieved when the Echarikith looked into her mind and found the Yajixa enslaved within.

The battle for the city had finally been won! She had saved many of the Echarikith and had even captured one of the Yajixa leaders. Now they had to prepare for what was to come. No doubt the Yajirans wouldn't let them take the rest of the planet so easily. Avala was also certain they would attempt to rescue their captured leader. They still had a long road ahead, but for now, she needed to celebrate and rest.

PART 3

-CORE-

17

INTERROGATION

"How do I release the Echarikith from their prisons?" Avala asked a second time.

The Yajiran woman before her, Empress Daebla, laughed in response. Ever since the events at the City of Bones and the capture of the Yajixa Empress, Avala had been spending every sleeping moment attempting to find a way to free the Echarikith in Daebla's mind. So far all attempts to break the device holding them were useless. Her usual approach of ripping them from the Yajixa's heart while in a mindscape had also failed. She was left with little choice; she would have to force Daebla to tell her.

"You think you're so smart!" the woman said, cackling. "The only reason I'm even here is because of those monsters. If that one hadn't gotten clever and used you like that, you would be my puppet. Why don't you ask her to do it for you?"

Avala looked at Entrallia. The Echarikith had insisted on ripping the knowledge out of the Yajixa's thoughts, but Avala had decided that would be a last resort. She was starting to think they would have to resort to it anyway .

"Entrallia, do you want to try?" she asked.

"Do you actually want me to rip the information out of her? You were so opposed to it before."

The Yajiran's eyes went wide. "What did she say? She can't possibly rip it out of me!"

Avala nodded, "Do what you will. I give up."

Entrallia approached the woman. "After all you put my people through, you deserve a far more painful end than having your thoughts dissected."

"Just try it, fiend! Just know that after what your people did to us, you deserved everything we did to you!"

As Entrallia began chanting in her ancient voice, Daebla's body seemed to unravel. Countless stands of thought flew out from her and formed a sphere. It appeared like Daebla was a ball of yarn that was being unwound until nothing was left. Finally, Daebla was gone.

Entrallia turned to Avala, her face a mask of rage. "This wasn't the real Daebla! She was a decoy! Though the real one is still enslaved, she is likely somewhere hidden within her mindscape. And since the mindscape still won't answer to your will, we are left with little option other than to search."

Avala nodded. It had taken them long enough to reach that point. Attempting to search the entire mindscape of a being that had been alive for three million years would take nearly as much time. It would take far less time to win the war with the Yajirans.

"We'll start looking," she said. They had no other options. To free those Echarikith, they needed the information from Daebla's mind-self or "Living Thought," as Entrallia called it.

She left the prison room and began walking the streets of her mind-city. She estimated that she had been wandering a good three thousand years in the distant past before she was brought back to her own time. In that period, her mindscape had grown massive.

She had learned that the souls inside a mindscape could still reproduce and still aged at least to adulthood. That accounted for some of the extra people and the families that had formed. Others, races she had never seen before, had been absorbed during her long wanderings. It seemed that life inside her mind was not all that different from reality, although sickness, hunger, and long-lasting injury were non-existent.

She discovered that her brother, Vran, had become a leader of sorts, even though he had not intended it. He had also gotten married to a woman around his own age during the Years of Wanderings, as people in her mind called it. They had eleven children, some of which had their own spouses and children.

All around her, people went about their daily lives. Though hunger was not an issue, many enjoyed eating, because it made them feel like they were still alive. It seemed that all complex lifeforms— what the humans called multi-celled organisms—were capable of being absorbed into her mind. This included plant life and animals. Also, every soul absorbed was again reborn into the mind after death. While a dead animal or cooked plant would stay dead while being eaten, they would reappear where they first entered the mindscape in a recreated body.

She entered part of her mind where the Drilik spiders had made their home. Over a long period of time, the spiders had been tamed, their webs now harvested for silk. Seeing them reminded her of how new building materials were found. Several deeper parts of her mindscape contained a wealth of portals to wild mindscapes, where resources were plentiful. Entrallia claimed these wild mindscapes must have come from Echarikith cast-offs who either lost sapience or lost life altogether, leaving behind only a mindscape.

It turned out that all descendants of Echarikith cast-offs had mindscapes. They were also all connected by something called the mindworld. However, getting to other sapient mindscapes often proved nearly impossible unless both parties agreed, because the portals were hidden from unwanted outsiders. It was not uncommon to meet inhabitants of other Yajixa minds within the wild mind-scapes, meaning they were also connected to them.

In general, non-Yajixa mindscapes contained only non-living things and echoes of memories. They served no real purpose. Thus when portals to them were discovered, they became refuges for souls trying to hide from something. However, entering the empty mindscapes was dangerous, because the portals could often disappear without warning. Thus, most people in her mind blocked any portals to empty mindscapes as soon as they were discovered, only entering to gather materials from ones that had proven safe

Avala found herself in a large chamber with many doors. She had shaped the place herself. She called it the Connection Chamber. Every door connected to one of the other mindscapes that she had connected to her mind, either by killing the Yajixa that once owned them or by linking them, as she did with Evyn and the Avalans.

As she thought of Evyn, she remembered how she had offered him a way to regain his power but still remain under his own control. He accepted gladly, since, being a natural coward, he feared death. He was also glad to replace the beating heart in his mind with an Echarikith crystal, because he found it disconcerting.

The Echarikith crystals, named for the actual beings, were empowered by Entrallia when Avala first willed them into being. The drone had placed minute portions of the Consciousness into them, which was still more than enough. This ensured they granted the same power that the enslaved Echarikith had provided, thereby removing the need to enslave them.

Avala walked to a well-guarded doorway in the Connection Chamber. The guards let her pass without question. It was the entrance to Daebla's mindscape. As she entered, she was greeted once again with the sight of the trapped Echarikith. Every creature that had originally inhabited Daebla's mind had either been freed, if they had been a slave, or captured, if they were loyal to Daebla. They had used the great prison rooms in Daebla's mindscape to detain the loyal ones, because it seemed an ironic punishment for them.

She walked up to the massive control station for the Echarikith soul cage. Nobody in her mind or any of the connected ones could figure out how it worked. There were over a million different controls, all of them unlabeled. This left them at a loss at how to unlock the Echarikith within. The best they could figure out was that it required pressing certain buttons in a specific sequence. However, due to the risk of what might happen if they pressed the wrong ones, nobody was allowed to touch the control panel. The area was guarded by at least a dozen warriors, all wearing the new symbol of the Avalans on their armor.

Behind the guards, a group of the brightest souls from her mindscape and the connected ones worked at deducing what each button did. Most of it was guesswork, since pushing the buttons was forbidden. After checking on them, she determined they still did not know how to release the Echarikith. She already knew they didn't, but checking was good for morale. It meant she believed they stood a chance at cracking the code.

She sighed and looked around the mindscape. The place was built like a fortress, defensible from nearly every location. The fact that Daebla's true mind-self was hidden somewhere inside proved that it also hid many secrets. Finding her was their top priority. Avala would have to get Vran to organize search parties.

She left the mindscape and then willed herself to what she called the Council Chamber. Once there, she sent a mental message to the Avalans to form a meeting. As each arrived, they took their seats around the table. Once all were accounted for, including Vran and Entrallia, who she had summoned with her will, she began speaking.

"Our interrogation of Daebla has proven futile. It appears the one we had locked up was an imposter, a puppet that was playing the part of the Yajixa. That means the real Daebla is in that mindscape somewhere, and we need to find her." Avala slammed her fist on the table. "This is our top priority. We can't release the Echarikith until she is found. To that end, we need search parties searching every nook and cranny in there. Every secret room or door must be found. The sooner we find her, the sooner we can free those Echarikith. The sooner we free those Echarikith, the sooner we win the war." She paused and looked around the room. "Any questions?" Nobody had any, so she nodded by way of dismissal. "That's all for now."

As the others began leaving, Vran caught Avala's attention. "Do you think it's possible for her to be hiding in your mindscape?" he asked.

She hadn't thought of that. It would be a perfect hiding spot, since nobody would check for her there. It was also possible that she had escaped to another part of the mindworld, maybe even a wild one. She frowned. "This worsens the problem. If she's not in her own mindscape, she could literally be anywhere. We know that countless portals were connected to hers." She shook her head, "We should still focus our search on her mindscape. We only have a limited amount of people to spare."

He nodded. "I'll organize the people. You should be waking up soon."

He was right. She could already feel her body begging to wake. It pulled at her mind-self, trying to tear her away from her internal work. It had been doing it for a while. Finally, she let herself drift to wakefulness.

As she woke up, she found herself once again in her quarters at the command center, but something was wrong. Not only was there screaming outside her room, blaring noises signaled an emergency. In addition, something or someone was slamming against her door, causing it to bend inward. She went to open it but then thought better of it.

"Adjutant. What's going on?" she asked in a shaky voice.

"It appears the Yajirans have attacked us," the Adjutant said calmly. "They claim to be searching for you. I would normally suggest handing yourself over to spare any more bloodshed, but I suspect they would still massacre everyone here. We are far too important to the Republic for our greatest enemy to spare us, so I suggest you defend yourself, since the door is at ten-percent integrity and is about to break open. Good day."

Avala picked up a beam pistol from beside the hearth and aimed it at the door, preparing to fire at whatever came through.

18

THE GIRL CALLED NAMJILA

When the door burst open, Avala fired. A Yajiran soldier fell to the ground with a burning hole in his chest. Avala felt a cold breeze flow toward her as another Yajiran stepped over his corpse. She fired again, but the soldier triggered an energy shield, blocking the shot. Stepping into the room, the soldier tried to grab her, but she dodged him. "Adjutant, MELT me to the LR-VRP! Now!" It was the safest place she could think of, not to mention the first place that came to mind.

"Confirmed," the Adjutant responded as the world around Avala began to melt away.

As the world came back into focus, Avala noticed something was wrong with the forest. The trees were all a sickly orange and red color, and the air was thick with a yellow fog. She coughed.

"You won't find safe refuge here, little girl." The teenage girl Avala had seen while in Empress Daebla's body walked out from between the twisted, malformed trees. "Impressive technology you have here. The things I can create."

"How does the Adjutant obey you?" Avala asked, coughing as more of the strange yellow fog choked her.

"Simple. I've absorbed the soul of your poor commander. When I channel her, the Adjutant can't tell the difference. Watch, I'll show you." She closed her eyes. The next time she spoke, it was in the voice of Commander Sylvia. "Adjutant. Create three Death Yannows from Yajiran mythology. Also, please bypass the safety protocols."

Avala was horrified. How had she killed Commander Sylvia? It couldn't be true. However, what the Adjutant said next informed her that something was not right. "Confirmed. Have a good day, Commander Elexia."

Before her eyes, seven creatures materialized. They looked like human-sized worms with arms and legs. They each carried a spear and wore heavy plate armor. They stared angrily at the girl.

"What? I asked for Death Yannows not Salimith from Egrogan mythology!" the woman cried, using her own voice.

"That is correct. Your voice pattern and life force may have momentarily been nearly identical to that of Commander Sylvia McCarthy, but it was more appropriate to her twin sister, killed four years ago by Yajixa. Due to simple logic, I deduced that you are, in fact, a Yajixa." The Adjutant sounded pleased with itself.

The seven creatures charged at the other girl with their spears aimed at her chest. "I like this body too much to leave it now!" She leaped into the branches of a nearby tree as the Salimith collided with each other. The girl pointed her hand at a nearby creature, and energy shot out of her fingertip, searing a hole in a Salimith's chest.

"By the way, my name's Namjila!" the girl said, smiling as she shot another creature. "And you are Avala, the child who captured my mother!"

Avala began backing out of the forest, but Namjila followed in the treetops. "What do you want?" Avala asked, though she thought she knew the answer.

"I want my mother's position! Isn't it obvious?" Namjila said as she fried another of the creatures.

"You don't want to free her?" Avala asked. She thought the Yajirans were there to free their leader.

"She's weak! She let herself get captured by a child! I intend to make certain she doesn't break free." Namjila's grin sent shivers down Avala's spine. "No doubt you've had trouble breaking her Living Thought. She was always so paranoid!"

Avala did not like this girl. Were all the Yajirans so corrupt that they would turn on their own parents? "How do you plan to stop her?" Avala asked, scared of the answer.

"Simple. I let you free the Echarikith inside her," the girl said, killing two more of the worm men.

"Why would *you* want to free the Echarikith?" Avala asked.

"Why? Because I have a far better power source!" Namjila replied with wicked excitement.

"A race from beyond this galaxy gave me incredible power once I absorbed it. It also frees me from my mother's will. I don't need the Echarikith anymore! They are weak compared to what I've enslaved."

Avala reached the edge of the forest, only to realize a metal wall barred her path. She began running along the wall. She needed to get out of there; the fog was making her dizzy.

"There's no point running, Avala. Once I'm done with these pests, I'm coming for you," the girl yelled.

Moments later, Avala felt her mind fog up, and she collapsed as the world went dark.

She opened her eyes. She was once again in her mindscape, but the yellow fog was there too. Everywhere around her, people were coughing and passing out. She looked around for any sign of the Yajiran girl but found nothing. Suddenly, she realized where Namjila must be.

She willed herself to the Connection Chamber and passed through the door leading to Daebla's mindscape. Inside she saw the massive device, with Namjila at the control center. The guards were all unconscious on the floor with traces of yellow fog around them. As Avala approached, a Yajiran woman appeared out of nowhere and ran toward the girl.

"Namjila, what are you doing? Get away from there!" the woman roared. Avala knew it must be the real Daebla. She also knew that if the real Daebla had come, then the Empress was in great danger.

"It's too late, *Mother*! You're not getting out of this!" Namjila shouted, pure malice in her voice.

Before Daebla could reach her daughter, the massive device trapping the Echarikith shattered, and an enormous rift into the void opened just outside. The Echarikith poured through in massive numbers, seeking freedom from their prison. Daebla's eyes went wide in horror. She slumped to her knees and began to weep.

"Goodbye, Mother!" The younger Yajiran cackled as she disappeared.

Avala walked slowly toward Daebla. The woman looked heart-broken. "Why would she turn on me?" Daebla cried. "We were so close. She's never been one to want power!"

"Are you okay?" Avala asked.

Daebla looked up at her with pure rage. "It's because of you that I'm in this situation! I may be a trapped soul here, but I will *not* cooperate with you!" She leapt at Avala with such force that she was knocked to the ground. "I'll kill you!" she roared as she tore at Avala, attempting to rip out her heart.

Avala willed Daebla off her, only to be attacked again. The woman seemed desperate to hurt Avala and did not seem to care if she hurt herself. After several long moments of struggle Avala managed to get out of the way. She used that time to her advantage, willing the other woman into chains.

Daebla struggled in the chains and roared in anger and frustration, tears streaming down her face. Avala almost pitied her. Here was a woman who had had all the power she could ever dream of, and it had just been stripped from her by someone she had trusted with her life. Avala knew that Daebla would most likely never recover from what had happened, though she hoped she would. Having the knowledge of one of the original Yajixa would be extremely useful in the war.

She sighed and walked toward the exit. As she entered her own mindscape, Vran stopped her to ask what had happened. Avala explained as best she could.

"I'll see that something is done with Daebla," Vran said once she had finished. "We'll go easy on her though. That's a horrible way to end, being turned on by her own daughter, who she obviously loved."

"Entrallia will want her to suffer more, no doubt," Avala said.

Vran nodded. "We'll see that Entrallia doesn't get her hands on her."

"What's going to happen now," Avala asked, "now that the Echarikith are free?"

"We continue the war. Although I suggest you try to avoid that girl for the time being. I don't think she's going to spare us next time."

Avala nodded. She still did not understand why Namjila had done what she had, but it was obvious that she would become a serious threat in the future. Avala could already feel herself awakening. She embraced the feeling as she fell into wakefulness.

19

THE PORTAL

As Avala opened her eyes, the distinct smell of smoke assaulted her nostrils. Sitting up, she noticed she was still in the LR-VRP, except now the forest was all burned down. Fortunately, she was still on the edge, where she had passed out.

Among the charred trees, she heard people calling her name. She recognized their voices as those of Alvaj and Commander Sylvia. She called out to them, and they were at her position in a moment.

"Are you hurt?" Sylvia asked, looking concerned.

Avala shook her head. "Where are the Echarikith that were freed?"

"You mean the ones you freed a few weeks ago or new ones?" Alvaj asked, looking puzzled.

"There were hundreds of them! They should be here!" Avala looked around, confusion and fear coursing through her.

"We haven't seen any new ones, dear," Sylvia said soothingly. "Then again, the attack ended hours ago. We've been cleaning ever since. We only came searching for you in here when we realized a fire had started with you still in it."

"How did you know I was in here?" Avala asked.

"The Adjutant told us you were here and that you were safe. That is, until the fire started, at which point the Adjutant was unable to locate you," Sylvia replied. "We're so glad you're alive."

Avala noticed that Alvaj was gaze at the ground with a look of amazement. When she followed his eyes, she saw an outline of ash and charred metal in the shape of her unconscious form. "How did you survive?" he asked, raising his eyes to her. "There's not a burn mark on you or your clothing."

Avala looked around, as if an answer would reveal itself. She did not understand it, but she suspected it had something to do with the Echarikith. Curious, she turned to Sylvia. "What started the fire?"

Sylvia shook her head. "We don't know, but whoever started it also turned off the Adjutant's fire-suppression system in the room. However, we found an unknown substance coating the walls and ceiling, which kept it unharmed by the fire. Whoever started it wanted to burn the forest and leave the rest undamaged."

"Why were you in here anyway?" Alvaj asked.

"I was trying to escape the Yajirans," Avala said, then explained what happened after she arrived in the LR-VRP room.

"Do you think the Echarikith started the fire?" Alvaj asked. "If the trees really were diseased and sickly, they may have destroyed it intentionally, not realizing there was a simpler way."

"Adjutant, what happened after Avala fell unconscious?" Sylvia asked.

"After Avala and the Yajixa fell unconscious, countless new life forms appeared on my sensors, indicating that someone found a way to use the LR-VRP independent of my control," the Adjutant replied. "However, many of these life forms are not in my database, which, I might add, includes nearly all known creatures, including those extinct and from fiction or mythology."

"What happened to them?" Alvaj asked.

"After they appeared, my sensors in the LR-VRP ceased to function. When my sensors came back online, I detected that a fire had started, and the smoke prevented me from detecting Avala. All data indicates that the sensor malfunction and the fire were caused by someone in the room. The only conscious beings at the time were the ones that had just appeared."

"Is it possible they were Echarikith?" Avala asked.

"Unfortunately, I cannot give a definitive answer," the Adjutant replied. "None of the known Echarikith give off any readings to indicate they are something other than what they appear. Thus my only answer is, yes, it is possible, but please take that with a grain of salt."

Avala cast a questioning look at Sylvia. "A grain of salt?"

"An old Earth saying. It essentially means take it with a bit of skepticism," Sylvia replied.

"I believe the Athakarin saying is, 'It didn't come from the Spirits'," Alvaj added.

Avala nodded, then returned to the subject at hand. "They must be the Echarikith that I freed, but where could they have gone?"

"Let's ask the Adjutant," Alvaj suggested.

"As I have said, I don't know what happened to them afterwards," the Adjutant responded drily. "There is no indication that they left this chamber through proper mechanisms, because the door was never opened. Also, I would have noticed if a multitude of strange creatures were moving through the complex, and I'm certain I would not be the only one."

"Any indication of another exit point?" Sylvia asked.

"Scanning . . .. There appears to be a large forced opening in the wall forty meters north of your position. It leads into maintenance tunnels in which I have limited sensors. I don't believe the opening was there before," the Adjutant added somewhat sarcastically.

Avala looked around. She could not tell which way was north. And apparently, neither could the other two, because they both started heading one way before the Adjutant spoke. "If you're seeking the forced opening, you are going the wrong way."

They turned around and started heading north, coming across the hole in no time. It was massive and precisely cut. It led to a dark tunnel going to both sides, its walls lined with pipes and wires, both of which Avala had only recently learned about. There were no lights inside and no indication as to which way the Echarikith went.

"Which way do we go?" Avala asked, looking as far as she could in both directions.

"First, we're going to need some equipment," Alvaj said. "Adjutant, prepare three sets of safety gear and three mobile Adjutant uplinks and scanners. And replicate any of the wearable items directly onto us."

"Agent Allan, if you are trying to flatter me by bringing me with you, I'm afraid it will not work," the Adjutant said almost mockingly as gear materialized directly onto the three of them.

"I'm just being practical. We will need your scanners in there," Alvaj said, chuckling.

"As I said, flattery will get you nowhere. Now please, do be careful. It may be dangerous in there," the Adjutant replied.

"We will," Sylvia said, turning to the tunnel. "Remember, follow my lead."

As they entered into the tunnel, the Adjutant pointed them in the right direction. "My sensors indicate that a massive number of creatures passed to the north."

Commander Sylvia nodded and began walking down the north tunnel, Alvaj and Avala following close behind.

As they walked, the Adjutant gave them directions based on its sensor readings. After some time, the Adjutant spoke up from the device strapped to Sylvia's waist. "Commander Sylvia, you may like to know that the Yajixa that was in the LR-VRP with Avala most likely had your twin's soul. The Yajixa was using her abilities to channel Elexia, giving her the authority to control the LR-VRP. Unfortunately, it took me some time to uncover this deception."

If Sylvia felt any sadness at being reminded of her lost sister, she did not show it. "So the reports that she had been killed by the Yajixa were correct. Serves her right."

Avala was shocked that the commander would say such a thing. "Don't you miss her?"

"Miss her? Yes. Remember her fondly? No," Sylvia replied. "She was the previous commander of Republic Intelligence. Her career ended when it was discovered she was sending agents to their death, so they would be absorbed by the Yajixa called Namjila. After her court martial, she was supposed to be sent to the penal colony on Tethas IX. Unfortunately, her MELT transport was intercepted by a Yajixa MELT trap. She was presumed killed."

Avala recognized that name immediately. It was the same girl who had just attacked her. Was she actually the same person? She decided not to ask, since most likely nobody there knew.

Sylvia sighed as they turned a corner. "She was always cruel, but she was also always better than me at everything, and that led to her to promotion to the position of commander. However, I was next in line, so I was given her position."

"I'm sorry to interrupt, but I'm detecting some strange readings up ahead—some kind of massive energy reading," the Adjutant said. "It's just around the corner, to the left."

They turned the corner and found a strange sight: a hole in the middle of the air, hovering over a device in the shape of a stone with an arrow on it. Inside the hole, Avala saw a beautiful field of flowers with some sort of bright light in the sky. However, something looked wrong with the grass.

"Adjutant, is this some sort of portal?" Sylvia asked.

"Visuals indicate such, but other sensors do not," the Adjutant replied. "The technology seems alien to me. I have nothing like it in my database. If you intend to go through, I suggest you let me modify these uplinks to use MELT technology connections. Therefore, I can interface with them in real time from a great distance, or bring along an Adjutant pad or wristband."

"Agreed, we need the uplinks. We'll need to access an Adjutant panel to modify them. Where's the nearest maintenance access point?" Sylvia asked, looking around.

"Directly to your right," the Adjutant said. "It appears to be the one outside Echniath and Elizba's quarters."

20

ECHARIKITH INSANITY

As Avala, Sylvia, and Alvaj stepped out of the maintenance tunnel, they nearly crashed into Echniath, who had been standing right outside.

"What were you doing in there?" she asked, terror in her voice.

"What's wrong, Echniath?" Sylvia asked.

Echniath quickly straightened up as if nothing had happened. "Nothing's wrong. I just hope you didn't go through that portal in there."

"We were going to," Avala said, wondering what the girl meant.

Echniath whirled around them to block the portal. "You can't go in there! It's not for you!" she yelled, a wellspring of emotion in her voice. "You're no better than the Yajirans!"

Echniath growled as Sylvia put a hand on the young girl's shoulder. "Why are you being so defensive of it, Echniath?" Sylvia asked soothingly. "You know we intend no harm to your kind. If going through there makes us as bad as the Yajirans, can you at least tell us why?"

Echniath began to cry, her body shaking violently as she stood with her arms wide, trying to block the portal. "That world is going to be our new core," she said through her tears. "Without a core we're vulnerable. We're most vulnerable when we are creating a core. You going there could ruin us. That's what the Yajirans did. They came to our core while it was in the process of forming. We invited them to take part, but they betrayed us. They brought that device, and none of us could even attempt to stop them, because we were so weak."

Avala knelt so her eyes were level with the young girl's and smiled. "We're not going to betray you."

Echniath looked at her with an ancient fear in her eyes. "Most of us don't trust the lesser races. We have no choice but to keep everyone away."

"Echniath, do you trust us?" Sylvia asked.

After a long moment, the girl nodded slowly. "But what *I* think doesn't matter. It will take at least one of your years for it to be complete. We can't let anyone near it during that time. Otherwise, things could go horribly wrong!"

"When did it start?" Alvaj asked.

"Only a short while ago." Echniath sighed. "The portal has to stay open though in case any other of our kind are freed. The more Echarikith we have, the faster the process will go."

"The portal's not safe here," Sylvia said.

"I was going to put it in my quarters, but the energy signature would have tipped off the Adjutant, so I was forced to place it in here," Echniath replied, still guarding the portal.

"Well, the Adjutant knows of it now," Sylvia said. "It will be safe in your quarters now."

Echniath's eyes suddenly when wide with horror. "What have we awoken?" she asked.

Avala noticed a distortion in the air moving away from the portal and quickly behind them. She was about to point it out when Echniath's eyes began glowing bright red. As the Echarikith let out a shriek in an alien voice, Avala felt herself passing out. The world around her went red, and she felt herself being dragged through the portal.

Avala awoke to find herself bound to a post high above the ground. Below her, countless strange beings were chanting in the ancient voice of the Echarikith. To her left was Commander Sylvia, and to her right was Alvaj. Both of them were in the same predicament, tied to posts high above the ground. They were just waking up as well. She noticed several other people tied to posts. She recognized many of them from the command center.

The sky was dark, and countless unfamiliar stars shone throughout the void. The ground was covered in some sort of grass, although much of it was long dead and looked almost like hair. She looked around in hopes of seeing an Echarikith she knew when she spotted Echniath standing directly below her, her eyes glowing red.

"Why are you doing this?" Avala cried. As she was about to continue, a voice screamed in her head, telling her to be silent. Something was wrong. Never in all the time she had known the Echarikith had she seen their eyes glow red when they chanted. And never had they shown others anything but kindness. She called out into her mind for Entrallia, demanding she explain what was happening.

This is not right! Entrallia said. She sounded scared. *They tried to use this world as a new core, but it's sick. I can feel it among them. The consciousness is in agony!'*

Is there any way to help them? Avala asked.

Yes! You need to sever the heart link! Entrallia replied, terror in her voice.

What does the heart link look like? As Avala asked the question, she found herself staring at a rod sticking out of the ground. It looked like a branch from a tree that had grown a hand-like shape around a red crystal. The crystal was pulsing, and Avala knew it must be the heart link. *How do I get to it?*

Leave your body! If you don't, we'll never have a chance! Try possessing someone near it. It will be difficult but not impossible. Then do what you have to!

Avala took a deep breath, closed her eyes, and willed herself to leave her body. The world around her changed, and what she saw terrified her. Each of the Echarikith appeared to have tendrils of fleshy energy coming from their heads, leading to the heart link. However, it was the world itself that scared her the most. It appeared to be a massive organism. She tried to ignore what she saw as she charged toward the heart link.

The Echarikith all turned to face her, looking directly at her spirit. Their chant forced her backward, keeping her away from the device. She fought against it, pushing as hard as she could, but they were too strong. She was forced backward, their chant drilling into her mind.

Avala felt something change inside, like a thousand people were pushing her toward the heart link. She felt as if her spirit would break apart, but bit by bit, she moved closer to the strange object. Soon she could almost touch it. Yet being incorporeal, she could not remove it. She forced herself toward a nearby Echarikith and pushed her way inside. It was even more of a struggle than the previous one. The more she tried, the more her spirit felt like it was being torn apart.

She nearly recoiled as Entrallia took control of her once again. The Echarikith spirit inside the body in front of her was displaced as easily as water as she fell into its body. Soon her new body was diving toward the heart link.

Her hands made contact, and searing pain shot through her as other Echarikith attacked her with their chanting. She tried to rip the heart link out of the ground, but it fought back, as if alive.

Her new body was being ripped apart, literally and figuratively. She fought against the voice and the object's will, trying desperately to remove or break it. Finally, she snapped the crystal off from the object. She was met with a scream of terror and pain that rang out throughout the landscape as the world itself roared in agony.

Earthquakes tore through the world, and she was ripped out of her new body and back into her own. As Avala looked through her own eyes, the ground parted into a giant circular maw filled with massive razor-sharp teeth.

The Echarikith, who appeared to be once again in their right mind, screamed as they plummeted into the gaping mouth. The post Avala was tied to also fell toward the great fanged gullet, and she could do nothing as she tumbled into the monstrous mouth. As she fell, the post snapped, and her bonds broke. She was in free fall, plummeting into the dark gullet of a world-sized beast.

Screams came from all around her as several waves of cool air blasted her. Finally, she landed on a squishy, slimy surface. The world came into focus once again, and she saw she was in a massive organic cavern, countless people strewn about the soft fleshy ground.

As the last people landed, a voice rang through the cavern. "Welcome. We've been waiting a long time for guests."

21

THE GREAT BEAST

Avala looked around the cavern, fear pounding in her veins. It was lit by some sort of organic lights. The only feature that stood out was a platform made of bone jutting out from an opening in the wall.

Not far from Avala, Echniath picked herself up. "No wonder we went mad! This world is actually a Chardrik!" she said.

Elsewhere in the cavern, countless people, both Echarikith and people from headquarters, attempted to stand. Most looked confused, afraid, angry, disgusted, or some combination of the above. Some, however, did not move, which explained the waves of cold air that she felt as she fell.

Commander Sylvia stormed toward Echniath, fury in her eyes. "You have a lot to answer for! So you better start explaining!"

Echniath sighed. "We're sorry about what happened." She looked at her feet. "The world we had chosen for our core turned out to be a Chardrik."

Sylvia gasped "Chardriks are extremely rare!" She looked around. "This definitely is one, but that still doesn't explain why you kidnapped me and many of my people!"

"When we began the process of connecting to the world's heart, we accidentally connected to the creature's mind," Elizba explained, walking over to them. "It seems to be suffering for some reason. That pain extended to all Echarikith and drove us mad."

"What stopped the madness?" Sylvia asked.

"I did," Avala said shyly.

Sylvia looked at her in confusion.

"She left her body, claiming one of our own, and destroyed the heart link device," Echniath explained. "Once it was destroyed, the link was severed."

"Then how do we get back to base?" Sylvia asked.

"We might be able to help with that!" a voice echoed through the chamber. Avala looked for its source and saw a worm-man, like the ones she had seen in the LR-VRP, standing on the bone platform. The Salimith was wearing a robe and holding a torch made of a bone with a glob of glowing green goo at the top.

"A Salimith?" Echniath said in confusion.

"Indeed, young one, we have waited a long time for the Echarikith to return," the Salimith said. "Though it appears you have accidentally brought along some mortals. We can help you return to where you came from, but first you must help us."

"What's wrong? Is it the same reason the creature is in pain?" Echniath asked.

"Indeed. The Yajirans have claimed part of the Chardrik and are mining it for resources." The Salimith looked sullen. "We have not been able to drive them out. They are looking for a way to the corestone. Once they destroy it, the Chardrik will die, and one of their emperors will absorb its soul."

"What's a Chardrik?" Avala asked, having heard unfamiliar term several times.

"They are creatures from another galaxy. Essentially, each one is a massive organism that encompasses a meteor or a small moon," Echniath explained.

"They are sapient and often draw lesser creatures into them to care for them," Elizba added.

"The most famous Chardrik in the Republic is the home world of the Egrogans," Sylvia said, seeming to forget her anger. "Though that one had been dormant for millions of years until about twelve hundred years ago. Before then, they didn't know it was actually a creature, since several kilometers of stone and soil had built up over it by the time the first Egrogans awoke."

"Yes, the world of Eneragas. That is one of the many Chardriks we were placed to watch over by the Echarkith so long ago," the Salimith said.

Alvaj walked up to him. "Since when did the Yajirans know enough about the Chardrik to be able to try and kill them?"

The Salimith sighed. "Since the one in the Terrion System was killed, about one Eneragas year ago."

"That's about half an Earth year," Sylvia said quietly.

"That project was led by a child of the Ten," the Salimith said angrily. "She killed it and absorbed its soul. Everything on that world died, though most of our kin had already been killed by the Yajiran."

Echniath looked at each of them in turn, as if silently asking them if they should help. Avala knew she wanted to help. As soon as Avala heard mention of a child of the Ten, she knew it was Namjila. Namjila had claimed she did not need to enslave the Echarikith anymore, because she had found a new source of power, one that came from another galaxy. It must have been one of the Chardriks.

Echniath turned to the Salimith. "We'll help."

"But you better help us get back afterward," Sylvia added.

"Thank you." The Salimith bowed. "Please, follow me. We will see that your dead are collected and your wounded healed. Do not worry about them."

Avala and the others in their small band climbed onto the platform, silently following the Salimith through the door and into the twisting organic tunnels. Avala was amazed at everything she saw along the way, including massive spaces with mountain-sized hearts, their heartbeats sounding like thunder. They passed through enormous rooms filled with forests of trees and gardens. The Salimith also led them across bridges over large pools of bubbling acidic liquid, which seemed to be digesting things.

Finally, they reached an area where the smell of smoke and burning flesh was apparent. Below them, under a ledge, was a massive area filled with countless different creatures, big and small, toiling under Yajiran taskmasters. They mined the creature's flesh and bones, hauling the material away through MELT tunnels. Huge tanks collected the creature's blood, pumping it from the mining areas. It was horrifying to watch. It looked like most of the creatures were slaves. Avala saw several of her own people, some of whom looked even younger than her. She felt tears in her eyes. How could they stop this?

"What's our plan?" Echniath asked.

"We break open one of those blood drainers and flood the place," Sylvia whispered.

"Most of those people are slaves," Avala said. "They'd drown."

"We could stage a revolt," Elizba suggested.

"The only ones here trained in undercover operations are Agent Allan and me," Sylvia replied.

"Yeah, but Avala could possess one of the Yajiran or a slave and help us that way," Alvaj pointed out.

"Elizba and I could easily pass as slaves as well," Echniath added.

"No, you couldn't," Sylvia said. "The Yajiran can tell what you are just by looking at you. Remember?"

"Then they could use their chanting," Alvaj suggested.

Elizba shook her head. "Won't work. The consciousness was wounded during the events on the surface. It doesn't have the strength to do what we need without major consequences."

Everyone was silent for a few moments as they attempted to figure out what to do. "Staging a revolt won't work," Echniath said finally.

"Why not?" Alvaj asked.

"They're soul slaves. Their souls have already been claimed by the Yajixa. Their bodies are just physical manifestations projected onto reality," Elizba explained.

"How do you know?" Sylvia asked.

"We see thing differently than you," the girls said simultaneously but did not explain further.

"Then drowning them isn't a problem, 'cause their already dead?" Avala said.

"Exactly," Sylvia replied.

"Then we need to break open those blood drainers and jam the shut-off valves," Alvaj said.

"We need to work fast, or else we'll get caught," Sylvia added, then looked at the two Echarikith. "Would more of your people be able to help us? It will make it easier."

The two young girls looked at each other, then nodded. "Sure, they'll be here soon."

22

OBVIOUS SABOTAGE

From the ledge, Avala watched the slaves below. The others were preparing to strike at any time. Nobody seemed to suspect anything. In a corner, she saw a distortion in the air moving toward one of the blood collectors. She had learned that the distortion was an Echarikith, who had made a body for itself that was capable of invisibility. Unless one knew what to look for, they were hard to spot. A battle cry sounded, causing several of the beings below to look toward it. As they rushed over to the noise, the sounds of battle broke out.

Out of a corner of her eye, Avala saw a long snake-like tentacle reaching for one of the blood collectors. In another area, a spider-like Echarikith climbed over the heads of the other creatures, moving toward one of the holding tanks. She also saw what appeared to be a rock with legs charge into a blood collector, shattering it.

Blood spilled all over the place with the destruction of the first collector. Slaves rushed over to close the valves, but a brute of an Echarikith charged and ripped the valve out of the device.

A second blood collector exploded, and Avala saw a distortion moving away from it. As the slaves moved to close the valves, a quick-moving female humanoid Echarikith leapt toward it, doing acrobatics in the air and severing the handle from the shaft with a wickedly sharp bladed tail.

The spider-like Echarikith covered the tank in a liquid that froze it, so when she knocked it over, it shattered. Slaves tried to turn off the valves, but they were covered in thick webbing.

Another blood collector started pouring out blood as several large tentacles tore it open, and ripping out the valves. The slaves hacked at the long appendages with their tools, but they seemed to be indestructible.

As the blood flow filled the chamber, the Echarikith retreated. The Yajirans and the slaves who had been fighting rushed over to try and stop the flow of blood, but it was no use. The blood level was already waist deep for the Yajiran, and many of the smaller slaves were already drowning. Avala felt sad for them, hoping the Echarikith were right that they were not truly alive anymore. She half expected to feel a breeze toward her indicating souls being absorbed, but she felt none.

As the blood level approached the ledge, Avala turned to leave, only to find her path barred by some sort of blockage. She realized it was to stop the blood from leaving the area, but it was preventing her from escaping.

Fear coursed through her veins. The blood level was rising quickly and there was no way out. She ran to the blockage and pounded on it, screaming for it to open. It did not budge. She looked behind her and saw blood slip over the ledge.

She screamed for help, hoping someone heard her. Her heart pounded as the blood lapped at her feet. She began to cry. She knew she would not truly die there, but she was not ready to lose her original body forever.

Avala slumped against the blockage as the thick red blood came up to her waist. It seemed hopeless. As she prepared to abandon her body, she thought back on everything that happened to her in that body, cherishing the life she had lived. As the blood rose to her chest, she closed her eyes, waiting for the end.

When the blood reached her neck, she was beginning to leave her body. Before she could, the blockage burst open, dumping her and the blood into the tunnel beyond, and then shutting moments later.

As soon as she realized she was safe, she screamed in joy at being alive. She looked around to see who had rescued her but saw nobody. She stood up, wringing out her blood-soaked clothing. She did not know how to get to the others, so she started down the tunnel, hoping she was going in the right direction, smiling all the way.

Eventually, she reached a large cavern filled with a horrible sight. Many of her friends and those she recognized as the Echarikith were in a cage made of bones. Surrounding the cage were nearly three dozen Salimith, chanting in what sounded like to a prayer of sacrifice. Nobody had seen her yet, so she hid behind a massive bone. The cage was sitting next to a large mouth-like opening filled with rows of teeth.

Avala watched in horror as the Salimith opened a door in the cage, grabbed one of its inhabitants, and threw him into the mouth. The person screamed as the mouth devoured him, and Avala felt the urge to scream herself. What were they doing? They had helped them! And now the Salimith were sacrificing them!

She had to stop it. She released herself from her body and floated toward one of the armed Salimith, entering his body. Once inside, she charged at the nearby Salimith, slashing them open with the spear in her hand. She would make the creatures suffer for turning on her and her friends.

She slashed one down its midsection, then cut the head off another. As a Salimith armed with a sword stabbed her in the chest, she leaped into her killer's body. She continued her purge, slashing at every Salimith she could. The rest scattered, because they were unarmed. She chased them down, killing them one by one. When she was the last one standing, she threw the body directly into the maw, leaving it at the last second as the mouth devoured it.

Back in her own body, she rushed toward the cage, forcing it open. Many of the people thanked her, but some of them looked at her with concern, afraid of what they had seen her do. The worst look came from Commander Sylvia.

"You butchered them," Sylvia said.

Avala felt guilt well up inside. "They were sacrificing you!" she said, trying to convince herself as much as Sylvia that she had done the right thing.

Echniath was crying. "Why did they turn on us? We did as they asked. Poor Zanji, I felt his spirit be devoured."

Many of the Echarikith were crying or fuming at the fact that one of their own had been killed. In fact, only the humans seemed concerned that Avala had butchered the Salimith.

"How do we get out of here?" Alvaj asked.

Elizba looked up from her mourning. "First we need revenge."

Avala was shocked at the pure hatred on the girl's face. She had never seen her with any such emotion before. Many of the Echarikith spoke up in agreement.

"We are going to kill this monster! The pain inflicted by the Yajirans has driven it insane!" Elizba roared in fury. "It's protectors are linked to its mind. If they wanted to sacrifice us, then that means this creature wanted to eat us!"

As she spoke, the entire world around them shook violently. Long tentacles reached out from the ground, grabbing people and pulling them into the floor. Screams echoed through the chamber. A tentacle grabbed Avala and pulled her deep into the floor. For a few moments, she couldn't breathe.

Avala opened her eyes to the sound of Echarikith chanting. It was coming from everywhere all at once. It sounded like an entire army's worth of people, all speaking in the same voice. The chanting echoed through the chamber she was in. She was floating in liquid in a dark cavern. It burned her body, as if eating away at her flesh. Something in the liquid tried pulling her downwards, and she screamed as she fought its grasp.

As the chanting grew louder, a roar of anger nearly drowned out everything else. Suddenly, a blast of ice-cold air hit her from all sides, freezing the liquid into crystal. Shortly after, the wind abated, and the chanting stopped.

A fog began to fill the chamber. When it touched Avala, she felt as if she were passing through a waterfall. The world around her shifted to a strange dream-like area. It appeared like she was standing on a glass plane. All around her were countless others, all from the giant creature. In the center of the plane, a massive sphere of darkness was quickly expanding. When it touched her, she passed out.

When Avala opened her eyes, she was lying in grass. Above her the sky was an odd blue color and was dominated by a strange bright object that hurt her eyes. She heard laughing and talking. All her friends were celebrating that they were alive.

She sat up and saw Echniath staring her. "You're awake!" Echniath said. "We're safe, but the Echarikith need a core soon or we'll all die!"

"Is that why we're here?" Avala asked.

Echniath nodded. "This is Axas V. It's an actual planet this time. We're going to turn it into our core. Unfortunately, the Yajirans have already detected us. They are en route to try and stop us."

"We don't have enough people to fight them," Avala said weakly.

"No worries. We made a portal to Ecrekio and gathered the other Avalans. We also opened a portal to the Republic's military head-quarters. Sylvia convinced them to provide some reinforcements

They can't give us much, but it will have to do. We were just waiting for you to wake up, so we could begin the ritual."

Avala nodded. "I'm ready."

23

THE BATTLE FOR THE CORE

Avala watched as Echniath placed the heart link into the ground. As the crystal at the top began to glow blue, she felt energy in the air. The Echarikith began chanting in their ancient voice, linking their hands together. She felt that this time they were not going insane.

The sun, as others had called it, was so bright that it made it difficult for her to see. Encircling the Echarikith were at least 120 human and Egrogan fighters. It was the first time Avala had seen the Egrogans. They were about the same height as the humans and her own people, but their heavy build and hunched back made them look bigger. The humans compared their heads to that of Earth creatures called turtles, which she had never seen before, so she couldn't tell if they were right.

A few Nerafin mercenaries were also among the defenders. Avala had been told the Nerafin were not official allies of the humans but merely trading partners. The Nerafin were traders and business folk by nature, and they had no love for the Yajirans. Like the Egrogans and the Yajirans, they were said to be descendants of the cast-offs of the Echarikith.

The Nerafin were fish-like humanoids. Their hands and feet were webbed, and their faces looked like fish. According to the humans, there were at least a hundred different types of Nerafin, each with its own head shape and scale pattern. Though they looked like fish, they could only breathe underwater for a few bell tolls before needing air again.

The Avalans were scattered among the other defenders. Those who had become skilled at looking into other beings' minds were watching the Echarikith cast-off races for signs of possession. If they discovered it, their job was to pacify the victims before they could do any harm to themselves or others. However, possession was unlikely due to a Mind Trap Field Generator, which the Republic had reverse-engineered from the Yajirans a few thousand years earlier.

A glint of light in the distance caught Avala's attention. Before she could figure out what it was, one of the Egrogan defenders dropped dead, blue blood spilling out from his head.

"Snipers!" Sylvia cried out. "Raise the shields!"

A massive energy shield sprang up around their area, its silver hue barely visible. Avala waited in suspense, watching what would happen. The suspense was broken as several massive metal spiders melted out of the ground in the distance. The Yajiran spider tanks bore down on their group, massive cannons firing at the shield. Each shell shattered when it hit the shield, showering the area around it with shrapnel.

Thousands of Yajiran soldiers and soul slaves came over a rise. Among them were massive, stupid-looking humanoid brutes pulling several of the spirit stealer devices. At the head of the army, nine Yajirans rode massive winged reptiles. Avala realized they were the remaining nine leaders of the Yajiran Empire.

She was overwhelmed with terror as she saw the forces arrayed against them. The odds that they would survive were impossible. The Echarikith could not help them, because they were focused solely on building their core. Thus, their defense force was tiny compared to the advancing army. The Yajirans were throwing everything they had at them. Avala knew they would stop at nothing to prevent the Echarikith from creating a new core.

The Echarikith had said it could take a year to complete the process. The chance that they would survive an entire cycle was low as it was; to survive an entire year was impossible! The only way to speed up the process was if more Echarikith could be set free.

A tenth winged reptile came flying down from the sky and settled alongside the others. Riding it was Namjila. When Avala saw her, something inside Avala snapped.

She's one of them now? Daebla roared inside her. *They turned on me! They will pay! I no longer owe them any allegiance or mercy! Throw us at them and I will aid you in destroying them!*

Avala felt Daebla's anger overtaking her, as if the Yajixa's former mindscape had turned into a furnace, fueling her anger. She also felt another massive source of power inside that she had never felt before. She flung herself out of her body with such force that it overcame the mind trap field. She flew through the air at one of the Yajiran leaders. As she reached them, she impaled herself into his mind.

She found herself in a void heading toward a fortress at incredible speed. The new power sources pushed her through the walls of the fortress. She broke through wall after wall, going faster and faster, nothing able to stop her. As she approached the center of the fortress, she saw a massive transparent sphere holding countless Echarikith in their natural form.

She was going too fast to stop, and she shattered the sphere as she plowed straight through it. She kept going, smashing through every obstacle. She broke through the other side of the fortress and into the void.

Once again, she flew through the air in the real world. Behind her, the Yajiran she had torn through slumped forward onto his mount, no longer moving. Ahead of her was one of the giant brutes pulling a spirit stealer device. She flew into it, possessing it. In her new body, she turned on the device, smashing it to pieces.

All around her, the puny Yajirans and other slaves turned on her. She smashed at them, felling dozens with each strike. In the distance, she saw the shield faltering. She roared, charging toward another spirit stealer, smashing into the brute pulling it. As she fought with the creature, she caused the device it was pulling to tumble through the area, damaging it and countless enemy forces each time it hit the ground.

She left the body and headed toward one of the spider tanks. She flew through the wall of the cockpit, taking control of the pilot. The new power sources within her allowed her to absorb the knowledge of the Yajiran in an instant. With this knowledge she began turning the cannons on the remaining spirit stealer devices, destroying them. Cannon fire began tearing into her own tank, but she kept firing. As the last of the spirit stealer devices was destroyed, she fled the body.

As she flew, the shield sparked one last time, then disintegrated. Countless wisps of energy flowed toward the defenders. Avala recognized them as other Yajixa; the mind trap field must have failed as well. She faltered. What had she accomplished? Her own body lay in the middle of the defenders, with Yajixa heading straight for it. She cried out as the Yajixa began possessing countless defenders, including her own body.

With anger welling up from her core at the sight of her body being controlled by someone else, she flew toward it with such speed, then she impaled herself once again into a Yajixa's mind.

She found herself in the mind of a child. Though some part of her wanted to kill the Yajixa, she knew she had to do the right thing. She flew toward the Echarikith slave chamber, crashing through walls and structures. With a thought, the Echarikith was replaced by a massive crystal. The mindscape answered her will, obviously due to the new power sources. She exited the mindscape after urging the child to take care of her body for the time being.

Once she was back in reality, she flew toward a possessed Egrogan. She forced her way into his mind, repeating the process she had done with the first one: tearing into the Echarikith slave chamber, replacing the Echarikith with the crystal, then leaving once it was done.

She flew out into reality once again, entering each Yajixa's mind in turn and freeing them and their Echarikith from slavery.

After the last was freed, there were way more Echarikith in the area than there had been when they started. The Yajiran army had reached the defenders, but the Yajixa she had freed showed their gratitude by attacking the Yajirans by possessing their own people. Chaos erupted within the ranks of the Yajirans as soldiers turned on others, and the tanks started blasting their own forces.

Up in the sky, nine of the winged reptiles flew in circles. Seeing the chaos, they flew away, melting into nothing moments later. An untold number of Yajixa suddenly abandoned their bodies and flew into the sky, following their leaders.

The Yajixa were gone, but the Yajiran army was still there, and they continued to fight. Avala returned to her body, which had been vacated for some time. As soon as she did, she felt something penetrate her mind.

Her eyes flew open to see something shooting through her mindscape. It appeared to be a person, but he or she was flying too fast to tell. People screamed in terror as buildings were destroyed. Avala rushed after the intruder, flying in her path. The intruder was heading toward a much deeper part of her mind, dealing as much damage as she could along the way.

Avala saw the intruder stop ahead of her. It was Namjila. She had stopped before a strange organic mass that covered the lowest portions of her mind. Avala stopped behind her, staring in horror at the mass of flesh. It appeared as if Avala had absorbed the Chardrik's soul. It was her new power source. Avala felt Namjila's intentions—she intended to destroy it in hopes of destroying her. Avala couldn't let that happen.

24

BATTLE AGAINST NAMJILA

Avala slammed into Namjila, knocking her away from the organic mass. She could not let the Yajixa kill her new power source.

"You are no better than me! Killing and absorbing one of these things!" Namjila yelled.

Avala growled in anger at the thought that she was anything like Namjila. "I'm nothing like you! Its pain caused it to go insane. The Echarikith only put it out of its misery!"

"Doesn't matter why it's here. I can't let you keep it!"

Avala felt rage from Daebla, and the power from the Chardrik filled her mental form. She summoned her armor and weapons, preparing for battle. "This ends here!" she growled.

"Indeed it does!" Namjila replied, summoning her own armaments.

Whereas Avala had a Kyati sword and leather armor, Namjila had a beam pistol and padded armor. In reality, Avala would not have stood a chance, but this was a mindscape. Things did not always behave as they did in the real world, and Avala was counting on that to help her win the battle.

She charged at the Yajixa, dodging a blast from the beam weapon. Her blade came down, but Namjila was no longer there. She had already moved out of the way at lightning speed and came up behind her. Avala sensed the beam weapon firing. Faster than she could have managed in reality, she turned and blocked it with her sword. She followed the block with a swing of the blade and a dive toward Namjila's legs.

Namjila moved out of the way, but Avala was prepared this time. She swung her blade with lightning speed directly into her opponent's path, slicing cleanly through her torso. Namjila flinched as her body melded back together.

"It will take more than that to best me!" she said, cackling as she fired her beam pistol at Avala's heart.

Avala barely managed to dodge it. As she prepared to retaliate, another beam caught her square in the chest. The pain seared through her, and she screamed. She attempted to will the pain away, but another blast hit her in the back of the head. The pain roared through her body; she was dying. There was no way someone could survive a blast to the head.

She was about to give up when she remembered this wasn't reality. She only felt pain, because she believed the wound was real. It took her a significant amount of effort to will the pain away, but eventually, it was gone, and so was Namjila.

Her nemesis was nowhere in sight. The organic mass below her hummed with energy, though something seemed wrong. She tried to sense what the matter was. The realization hit her hard. Namjila had not fled but had decided to continue her objective. Avala cursed her foolishness and willed herself to Namjila's position.

She found herself in an enormous organic chamber. A large crystal floated in the center of the room, tangled in tendrils coming from the walls. Next to it was Namjila, also caught in a tangle of organic tendrils. She was screaming in terror as they attempted to rip her apart. It reminded Avala of what Entrallia had done to the fake Daebla.

Namjila looked at Avala with pleading eyes as the massive creature slowly destroyed her. Avala was filled with pity. Even though Namjila was one of the worst people she had ever met, she did not want anyone to be destroyed like that, not anymore. "Let her go!" she yelled.

The tendrils released the girl almost instantly. Namjila collapsed to the ground.

"Leave now!" Avala demanded.

"I didn't expect to survive that," Namjila said, chuckling. "But don't think this makes us friends. One day I will end you." She slowly disappeared.

Avala felt herself waking up as well. The world around her seemed to catch on fire as her eyes closed.

When Avala opened her eyes, she found she was back on the battlefield. The battle was over, the wounded were being treated, and the dead were being packed up for a final journey back to their families. The Echarikith were still chanting in their ancient voice, their words barely understandable but surprisingly beautiful.

Several people noticed she was awake and rushed over to her. She recognized some of them. Among them were Alvaj and Sylvia.

"You're alive!" Sylvia cried.

Avala smiled weakly, "I was attacked by that girl again. She was trying to kill me."

"Well, you survived." Alvaj sighed. "That's what matters."

"Who are all these new people?" Avala asked. Many of them appeared Yajiran, some as young as children.

"They're Yajixa who have been freed from the ten," Alvaj replied.

"Many of them believe you were the one who freed them," Sylvia added, smiling.

"More Avalans then?" Avala asked, chuckling to herself.

"Indeed," Sylvia replied.

As she said it, the world began to tremble, and a low hum arose from the ground. The Echarikiths' chanting became more fevered, and strange lights started dancing across the sky. The air became charged with some sort of energy, causing sparks to come of off random people and objects.

Avala felt terrified that this was some new attack by the Yajiran. All around her people were attempting to understand what was going on. Several people screamed as tendrils of energy shot up from the ground grabbing the corpses of the enemies and tossing them about. Blades of grass began turning into flames, igniting anything they touched.

The sky went dark, but no stars were visible. Something that sounded like a blast of a great horn sounded from the sky as jets of fire shot up from the ground. Massive bolts of lightning crashed down from the sky, staying where they were instead of dissipating. The ground began to buckle as pillars of stone shot up from it. Myriad massive tornadoes tore up everything in their path in the distance. The only place that seemed safe was a circular area around the Echarikith, which encompassed everyone among them. It seemed that the Echarikith were the eye of the storm, and all this chaos was their doing.

Avala watched in awe and terror as the world around them was reshaped by the chaos. Numerous towers of stone and metal pushed out of the ground, growing as if they were living things. Distant mountain ranges were leveled, while fields of grass were wiped away.

Stones ripped out of the ground and assembled themselves together, the Echarikiths' magic merging them into buildings and other structures. Metal tore from stone and began shaping itself, adding to the self-forming buildings. Trees began growing from the ground at a rapid rate, only to be torn apart, the wood cutting itself and adding to the structures. Sand ripped out of the ground, melted in midair, then formed into glass shapes, adding to the structures.

Roads made of colorful stones torn from the ground started molding themselves between the structures. Trees with beautifully colored leaves began growing along the edges of the roads, stopping at a manageable size.

As the building took shape, countless balls of light above the ground, coalesced into creatures of all types. Each one of them joined the chanting Echarikith, causing the sound to emanate from all sides. The city grew outwards from where they were, expanding into the horizon.

After what felt like an eternity of wonder and amazement, everything began to calm down. The Echarikith stopped chanting and looked around in awe. Avala looked at Echniath, who seemed happier than she had ever seen her. This world was now the core of the Echarikith.

Avala approached Echniath and Elizba. "Is it finished?" she asked.

They nodded in excitement. "We have our core once again! New Echarikith drones can come into being now, and we have a world to call our home." Elizba sighed and smiled.

"Now what?" Sylvia asked, walking up to them.

"Now we work on rescuing our kin," Echniath said.

"That won't be easy," Sylvia replied. "There are billions of Yajixa still out there, and they aren't going to go down without a fight."

"Then we fight," Echniath said. "Whatever it takes!"

Name and Terminology Dictionary

(THIS SECTION MAY CONTAIN SPOILERS.)

Adjutant: One (or multiple) self-aware AI(s) hired by the Republic of Earth Intelligence Service. Hired to act as aides to all personnel within Republic Intelligence Service Headquarters.
Alvaj (Al-vah-jh): Code name of Agent Allan (Ah-Lan). Human man. Spy for the Republic of Earth. Former husband of Avala due to forced marriage during his period as a spy.

Athakarin (Ath-ack-uh-rin): Half-human/half-Yajiran. Appear human in every way other than round eyes with slit pupils and a bigger range of hair colors. Blood is orange. Primitive people of planet Evelon II. Worship the "spirits," which are actually the Yajixa.

Athakri (Ath-ack-ree): Rebel Yajirans who revere the Echarikith.

Avala (Ah-vah-lah): Main character. Fourteen-year-old girl of the Athakarin race. First Yajixa freed from the Ten. Hometown of Childya. Gold hair, amber eyes.

Avalan (Ah-vah-lan): Former Yajixa who get their power from sources other than enslaved Echarikith. Avala is the first Avalan.

Avli (Av-lee): A Majiril guardian of Hideout: Yaji.

Avraintix (Av-rain-ticks): Great city close to the day side of Evelon II. Ruled by Fire King Vluad.

Axas V (Ax-ass): Fifth planet of the star Axas. Once an uninhabited planet, now the new core of the Echarikith.

Bell Toll: Measurement of time on Evelon II. One bell toll is about two hours.

Birth Rings: Seven rings made for every newborn Athakarin. Each one represents something about their birth.

Chardrik (Char-drick): A massive sapient organic creature from another galaxy. Begins growing on an asteroid or small moon. Produces breathable air around and inside it.

Childya (Chill-dyah): Hometown of Avala. Small backwater town close to the night side of Evelon II.

Crescent of Zayil (Crescent of Zay-yil): Name of the Moon of Evelon II.

Cycle (Evelon II): One cycle is twelve bell tolls. During each bell toll, the bells around a town ring once more than the previous bell toll, resetting after the twelfth toll.

Daigix (Day-gicks): Priest of Childya. One who sacrificed Vran. Body of the Yajixa, Yvan (Ee-van).

Empress Daebla (Day-blah): One of the ten original Yajixa and member of the Yajiran High Council.

Devalra (Deh-val-rah): Athakarin term for evil spirits. Essentially, humans.

Drilik Spider (Drill-ick): Ten-legged spiders of Evelon II.

Echarikith (Ehh-char-rih-kith): Ancient race of immortal beings that created mortal bodies for their drone spirits to inhabit. Has overarching consciousness that connects all drones. Disappeared three million years ago. Had entire race stolen from bodies by the first ten Yajixa. Natural form (only possible inside a mindscape) appears as giant skeletal-like creatures.

Echarikith Ancient Voice (Ehh-char-rih-kith): An alternate voice that is identical for all Echarikith. Words spoken in this voice have power. Known as the "Voice of the Consciousness" by the Echarikith.

Echniath (Ech-nee-ath): Member of the Echarikith race. Currently in the body of a little Yajiran girl. First Echarikith freed by Avala.

Ecrekio, the City of Bones (Ehh-creck-ee-oh): Underground city on Evelon II. Part city, part tomb, part ancient ruins of the Echarikith. Home of the Echarikith Walls of Prophecy.

Egrogan (Ee-grow-gan): An allied race of the Republic of Earth. Heavy build, humpbacked shoulders, turtle-like head.

Elexia (Ehh-lecks-ee-ah): Commander Sylvia's identical twin sister. Former commander of Republic Intelligence. Killed by Yajixa years ago.

Elizba (Ee-liz-bah): Member of the Echarikith race. Currently in the body of a little human-like girl. Second Echarikith freed by Avala.

Eneragas (En-err-ah-gas): Home world of the Egrogans. A Chardrik covered in kilometers of rock and soil. Was dormant until a thousand years ago.

Entrallia (En-trah-lee-ah): Member of the Echarikith race. Currently lives in Avala's mind within the body of a fourteen-year-old Athakarin girl. Looks identical to Avala, except has red hair and red eyes.

Eternal Fire: The day side of Evelon II. West of Childya and Ecrekio. East of Avraintix.

Evelon II (Ehh-veh-lon): Second planet of the star Evelon. It is tidally locked. The same side always faces the orbiting body. Only habitable area is a ring along the eternal sunset. Home world of the Athakarins.

Evyn (Ehh-vin): Former Yajixa, whom Avala freed and then linked to her mind.

Frozen Wastes: The night side of Evelon II. East of Childya and Ecrekio. West of Avraintix.

Heart Link: A device used by the Echarikith to create their core. Appears as a living stick with a crystal at the top.

Hideout: Avli (Av-lee): A cavern hideout on Evelon II inhabited by Athakri. The cave is guarded by a robotic or holographic "spirit beast" called Avli.

Human: Bipedal race from Earth. Originated long after the fall of the Echarikith. The main species of the Republic of Earth. Cannot be possessed by Yajixa.

HVRP: Holographic Virtual Reality Platform, a room that can create an illusion of being in different locations and situations.

Hydra III: Third planet orbiting the star Hydra. Home to the command center for the Republic of Earth Intelligence Service.

Ijar (Ee-jh-ar): One of the five eldest Yajixa on Evelon II. Currently possessing Fire King Vluad (Vloo-add) of Avraintix.

Ijix Bow (Ee-jh-icks): Bladed bow used by Yajirans and Athakarins.

Jindyo (Jind-yo): Yajiran slave husband of Empress Daebla.

Jira (Jeer-rah): Female Athakri. Security chief of Hideout: Avli.

Knakta Crystal (Kh-nack-tah): A type of crystal from Evelon II. Comes in different shades, including red.

Kyati Sword (Kh-yah-tee): A sword with a wide center part of the blade, capable of blocking arrows. Used by the Athakarins.

LR-VRP: Life-Replicating—Virtual Reality Platform. A secret project, similar to the HVRP, except it can create actual living beings. Based on reverse engineering of Echarikith technology.

Majiril (Mah-jh-ih-rill): An Athakarin spirit beast.

MELT Scan: A form of long-distance scanning using MELT transportation technology.

MELT Transporter: A form of long-distance transportation capable of transporting people and objects almost instantly between two star systems with very precise accuracy.

MELT Tunnel: Similar to MELT Transporters except it works automatically upon something entering it.

Mind Trap Field: A field that is supposed to prevent Yajixa from leaving or possessing bodies.

Mohavji Necklace (Moe-hav-jh-ee): A type of necklace worn by Athakarin women.

Namjila (Naym-jh-ee-la): Supposedly young, teenaged Yajiran Yajixa. Daughter of Daebla.

Nerafin (Nayr-rah-fin): Race of fish people. Can only breath underwater for a few hours. Traders and mercenaries. Informal allies of the Republic of Earth.

Noochi (Noo-chee): Member of the Echarikith race. Currently in the body of a male half-bat/half-man creature.

Northlands: Northern country of Evelon II. Known for its magics. Capital is the City of Trees. Ruled by Mage Queen Yamlai.

Orrain (Or-rain): Male Athakri scholar. From Hideout: Avli.

Salimith (Sah-lih-mith): Worm people from Egrogan mythology. Turned out to be not so mythological. Appear to be human-sized worms with arms and legs.

Soul Slave: A slave of the Yajixa whose soul has already been absorbed by the Yajixa but whose physical body is still animated by a projection of its soul.

Sylvia, Commander: Human female. Commander of the Republic of Earth Intelligence Agency.

Terrion System: (Tayr-ree-on): Star system where Namjila killed and absorbed the soul of a Chardrik.

Tethas IX (Teh-thas): Location of a Republic penal colony.

Vaix Dart (Vay-cks): Poisoned dart used by the Athakarins. Thrown from a sling.

Vran: Avala's brother. Young adult Athakarin. His soul lives in Avala's mind.

Wrakta Beast (Rack-tah): A beast of burden of Evelon II.

Yagra (Yah-grah): One of the five eldest Yajixa on Evelon II. Currently possessing Amalix (Ah-mah-licks), wife of the Fire King.

Yaji (Yah-jh-ee): Athakarin term for good spirits. Essentially Yajixa and Yajirans.

Yajiran (Yah-jh-eer-ran): Humanoid species. Has chains of scales instead of hair. Eyes are large with slits for pupils. Blood is golden. Came about due to cast-off bodies of the Echarikith.

Yajiran Spider Tank (Yah-jh-eer-ran): An eight-legged spider-like metal armored vehicle. Has a cannon on top and only one pilot.

Yajixa (Yah-jick-sa): Group of individuals who can transfer their consciousness to new bodies by "possessing" them. Can also absorb the souls of living things that die near them. Almost all are slaves to the original ten Yajixa. Draw their power from enslaved Echarikith.

Yasal (Yah-sal): Leader of the five eldest Yajixa on Evelon II. Currently processing Mage Queen Yamlai (Yam-lay).

Yvan (Ee-van): One of the five eldest Yajixa on Evelon II. Currently processing Daigix (Day-Gicks).

Zanji (Zan-jh-ee): An Echarikith whose soul was consumed by a Chardrik.

Zayil (Zay-yil): One of the five eldest Yajixa on Evelon II. Currently unknown who he is possessing.

Printed in Canada